THE
WOMAN WHO LIVES
IN THE EARTH

THE
WOMAN
WHO LIVES
IN THE
EARTH

ဢ ဢ ဢ

SWAIN WOLFE

HarperCollins*Publishers*

This book was originally published in 1993 by Stone Creek Press.

HarperCollins books may be purchased for educational, business, or sales promotional use. For information please write: Special Markets Department, HarperCollins Publishers, Inc., 10 East 53rd Street, New York, NY 10022.

FIRST EDITION

Designed by C. Linda Dingler

Library of Congress Cataloging-in-Publication Data

Wolfe, Swain.
    The woman who lives in the earth : a novel / Swain Wolfe.
        p. cm.
    ISBN 0-06-017411-0
    1. Women—Fiction. 2. Droughts—Fiction. I. Title.
PS3573.05257W65 1996
813'.54—dc20   95-36013

96 97 98 99 00 ❖/HC 10 9 8 7 6 5 4 3 2 1

For Sarah, Lynne, and Mother Wolfe

CONTENTS

୭ ୭ ୭

THE
WOMAN WHO LIVES
IN THE EARTH

In an unknown time, in an unknown land
the dark smoke of fires obscured the
savage masks that hid the fearing men.

A windlass sang its ancient song
beneath the burning sun
and a child studied the thin
and rainless clouds for signs of rain.

1
STONES

§ § §

Sarah rose up through the dry sage and the shimmering heat as she climbed the hill toward her father and the huge horse. She carried a pail of water and a bundle wrapped in dark red cloth. Where the sagebrush ended and the plowing began she stopped to poke at the fresh earth with her bare foot. For a moment she peered down at something hidden in the ground, then continued across the new-plowed furrows to where her father waited. She turned and looked back. "Something strange is buried there, near the edge of the field," she said.

He took a drink from the waterskin and studied her dark, almond eyes and her burnished cheeks. Perhaps she was teasing. "Is it stone?" he asked, as the field did not lack for stone.

His dry, skeptical tone brought a wry smile to her

face. "Yes," she said, "it's made of stone, but it's not like the others."

He was large and strong. A piece of faded red cloth covered his head like a small turban. His face, darkened by the sun and dirt, made the white of his eyes bright and intense. To a stranger he would be a crazy man, but to Sarah he was her father, who was Aesa, a farmer covered with the dirt of his field.

They ate their lunch of goat cheese, black bread, and boiled eggs. Horatio the plowhorse drank from the pail.

Sarah watched her father and wondered what it felt like to be so tall and strong, to leave deep footprints in the soft dirt of the plowed field. But he had no words for his life and that made him a mystery to her.

He blocked the burning sun from his eyes and studied the hot, dying hills to the west. Never had so much died for lack of rain. He drank from the waterskin, spilling the cool water over his lips and down his neck. The pure taste, the clean stone smell, and the simple joy of drinking water brought a thought into his head that was completely new to him, and dreadful. He peered into the mouth of the waterskin and asked, "What would happen if . . . ?" but he stopped. He stared out across the field, searching for another thought.

Sarah heard something in his voice, something

small but sharp. She insisted: "If what, Father?"

He said nothing. She looked at him, demanding the "if what." His dark eyes looked into hers and he said, "If our well went dry?"

"No water at all?" she asked. He answered with a nod so slight she barely noticed.

There was always water in the well. She watched the horse, his muzzle pressed firmly against the bottom of the pail, savoring his last drink until evening. "Horatio would be thirsty," she said, making a game of her father's question.

"Yes," he said. "What else?"

"We'd all be thirsty. The garden too."

"And what happens if the garden dries up?"

"Plants die." She gouged a furrow with her heel in the dry earth and thought about the green garden. She studied his eyes for signs of play.

She found only the serious, dazed eyes of a farmer in a drought. His voice searched for the thread of his thoughts: "When it rains . . . some goes like a mist . . . into the air . . . and some goes through roots . . . to plants. But some goes deep into the ground. Where do you think it goes?"

"Rain goes into our well?"

He nodded and ate his lunch and let her have her thoughts.

She wrapped her sinewy arms around her knees and

rocked back and forth with her toes. Finally she asked, "How does the rain find the well?"

"We dug the well to where the water flows."

She looked at the plowed ground between her feet: "You mean there's a river deep down?"

"Yes, like a river." He reached down and pressed his hard callused hand into the dry earth, then looked up at the sky. "There's been no rain for a long time."

She was embarrassed that she knew so little about the well. She tried to picture the river underground and waited for her father to finish what he meant to say.

Finally he said, "I don't think the well will go dry, my pretty child."

The words "my pretty child" stuck like thistles in her thoughts and made her feel small. She stood, long-backed and straight, and felt the warm earth under her bare feet. She looked at him. "If it doesn't rain on the field we won't have grain for bread or porridge. What will we do if there's no rain?"

Aesa had not expected this. He wondered how little he knew his daughter and said the simple truth, "We'll have to leave."

"Where will we go?" she asked.

"I don't know," he said and hoped his desperation was not carried in his words.

She pretended to hear what he wanted her to hear:

a heart so confident that it could say "I don't know," and feel no fear. "We could go to your grandmother's, couldn't we?" she asked.

He looked down at her and smiled and, in a dreamy way that made her laugh, he said, "Yes, that's just where we'll go."

She watched the huge horse sniff at his empty pail. The dark patterns of loam and sweat on his neck and flanks revealed a story of muscle bound to bone. She walked through the dry dirt, patted his silky muzzle, and rubbed the horn nubbin between his ears.

She tied her fine black hair behind her head with the red cloth, picked up the empty pail, and crossed the plowed furrows, pushing clods into the loose dirt with her heels. At the edge of the field she stopped and looked down at the thing hidden in dirt: a straight, black edge of stone.

"A slate," she thought, like her own, though much larger—more than four times the length of her foot and nearly as wide. She knelt down and dug the dirt away with her hands. Near the top on one side was a long, gray gouge that ended at a chipped edge. This mark seemed clean and new. She decided it was made by her father's plow.

Below the gouge she felt, then saw, a strange thing that made her eyes widen: letters cut in stone—a curious kind of writing she had never seen. The shapes of the letters reminded her of bean vines and pea pods. And there were slashes like the thin red petals of flowers that grew among the sage. She dug deeper as her head filled with thoughts of what it said, what kind of people put it there, what became of them. Maybe they hid in the hills, living in caves. "They could be watching." Her heart pounded with her thoughts.

She discovered the words were carved in a large circle and inside the circle was another, thicker circle of words. Several small, shallow holes were carved inside this second circle. And the sun grew hotter and the dirt harder. Her hair stuck to her forehead, dirt clung to her plain muslin dress, and the people hiding in caves receded from her thoughts. Finally her sore fingers made her decide it was worth a trip down to the shed for a shovel.

She stood at the field's edge looking down over the crest of the sage-covered hill. From there she could just see the top of the doorway to the farmhouse. West of the house was the garden with its high rail fence to keep the deer out. And twenty long steps to the east was a large shed, with its forge, tools, bins of grain, and the necessary shovel. Between the shed and the garden was the well and its windlass frame.

Below the house the land sloped down toward a dense grove of juniper trees and emerged on the other side as the rock ledge of a mesa. The hidden mesa looked out over a narrow canyon and far to the south and west was a range of high, sharp mountains—solid blue and flat as paper cut out and pasted against the sky.

As she descended the hill her father's words filled her mind: "I don't think the well will go dry, my pretty child." The words repeated themselves, rolling over and over like stones in her head. They rolled down the path through the sagebrush and far back into the dark interior of the shed. The words gradually came to a stop as she searched for the shovel. After her eyes could see in the dim light, the shovel appeared, but when she turned to go she was blinded by the patch of bright rectangular light that was the doorway and beyond it the yard. In the middle of the light, in the middle of the yard, stood the well, glowing in the bright sun.

For a moment it seemed as though the well would disappear, as though the stone wall and the windlass poles would waver and fade away, leaving only the patch of bright light framed in the dusty darkness of the shed. She walked toward the light, which grew larger and larger until she was standing in the doorway. As her eyes adjusted to the brightness she watched the well become real again. She wondered if there was a way to know if it was going dry.

Sarah walked out into the harsh light and up the

hill through the sage to uncover the mysterious words hidden in dirt. She worked the awkward shovel into the reluctant earth. As she dug deeper and deeper into the dry dirt the lack of rain became frightening—it was as dry two feet down as it was on the surface.

She stopped digging and used her sore, dry fingers to feel near the base of the stone slate for the slightest trace of moisture, but there was none. She could only feel that sharp edge of fear she had heard in her father's voice.

Far across the field the plowman watched his daughter struggle with the large, unwieldy shovel. She managed to dig the slate free of the earth's grip, but it was too heavy and she could not lift it. She waved to him, pointed to the slate, and then toward the house. He waved back, meaning that he would bring it, whatever it was, when he came home in the evening. And he wondered what could possibly be so important to her.

As she walked down the hill toward the farmhouse she remembered when she was little, asking her father what he grew in the field above the house. "Stones," he replied, in a voice that convinced her that stones needed growing. He pointed to the well and said that its wall was made of heavy stones that rolled down from the field. All by themselves.

She peered into the darkness of the well and

inhaled the cool air and the scent of wet stone. She climbed up on the wall, braced against the windlass frame, and looked straight down. To her surprise she saw a small patch of something bright and blue shining through the darkness, and something moving, sliding over the bright blue light. When she called "Hello," it answered back, "Hello," and when she laughed, its laughter rang back and forth with her own.

She had never stood on the wall in this very place and looked straight down into the water, so she had never seen herself or the sky reflected back. The reflection, she realized, would help her measure the exact water level each day, but first she had to find a way to mark the rope.

She climbed down and walked to the shed to fetch a piece of charcoal. When she returned to the well she loosened the windlass and let the bucket down and down until it just touched the sky to blur the blue light. Then she marked the rope at a point where it wound around the windlass, and she marked the windlass, too.

2
DREAMRAKERS

§ § §

Sarah's mother, who was Ada, stood in the doorway of the farmhouse and watched her daughter's long, evening shadow draw water from the well. Ada had milkmaid's shoulders, large hands, and legs like oaks. She had a small smile and playful eyes that challenged silly thoughts.

She watched Sarah's long shadow-shape turn the shadow windlass, draw the shadow bucket, and fill the shadow pail.

Sarah carried the pail to the garden. The water seeped deep into the waiting earth, turned it black and silky, and as she watched she could feel it seeping into her mind. She was lost in these sensations until the sound of her name floating in the air above brought her back to the world. Her father came down the path from the field and the slate-with-words lay across Horatio's broad back.

Aesa's tired face was a mask made of dirt with white-rimmed eyes. When he reached the yard he slowly eased the stone slate to the ground and set it against the well.

Sarah came with a small stick and sat on the ground and began scraping the dirt from the chiseled letters. "What does it say, Father?" she asked the large figure who loomed against the evening sky.

"Don't know that," he said.

"What is it for?"

"Don't know that, either. Never saw a thing like it. What d'you think?"

She squinted at the strange words and pretended to read: "This hard old pillow belongs to a very old woman who flies through the air all night and sleeps in the ground all day."

He looked at her with a serious face and said, "Yes. That's just what that says."

Ada came to investigate. She bent down to touch the slate, ran a finger over the strange letters, then she grasped it in her hands and turned it to the light. "Long ago people must have lived here. Were they farmers like us, do you think?"

Aesa shrugged. "What else?"

"Herdsmen? Maybe there was grass then." And she waved her arm at the sage. "How's the field?" she asked.

"Finished," he said, with a tired smile.

She stroked his dirty face. "Come with me," she said and led him to the bench in front of the farmhouse.

A ritual began. He removed the faded red cloth from his head then leaned far back as Ada gently pinched his nose and slowly poured a pitcher of water over his face and neck. Then she sat on his lap, untied his shirt, and washed his arms and chest.

Sarah leaned against her father's shoulder and watched the water spill onto the powder-dry earth.

𝔰 𝔰 𝔰

Their farmhouse was stucco-white, muted with a fine coating of dirt blown down from the field. Lime mortar was troweled flat over long poles that left a pattern of pale gray lines running the length of the walls. The few windows were thick glass slabs with bubbles and twists that changed the shapes of people and animals and mountains and clouds.

The roof, where Martha the goat spent her nights, was sod and nearly flat. Martha kept the grass trimmed short, and the sun kept it a pale yellow. Sometimes Sarah carried water up the ladder to the roof and turned the grass green again, and it would grow again, and Martha would trim it back again.

Inside was a table made of thick planks, chairs made

of smooth, thin branches, Ada's loom, a large trunk, an iron stove, shelves, cupboards and bins, a bed for Sarah, another for Ada and Aesa, a badger, two raccoons, a fox, several deer and six leopard skinks carved and painted on posts and beams and cupboard doors—the work of Ada when she was pregnant, first with Sarah and later with the boy who died when he was little.

On the south side of the house three thick windows looked out toward the distant mountains. A sage-covered slope dropped away from the house for about one hundred of Aesa's long steps to the grove of junipers and the hidden mesa. Far below the mesa a twisting creek snaked through a forest of cottonwood trees. Deer lived there.

§ § §

Dinner was bread, goat cheese, and crooked yellow roots dipped in a pot of something black and eaten raw. The utensils consisted of wooden spoons and iron knives. Instead of forks, they used elegant hinged grippers that resembled cranes.

Sarah held her cup over her head: "Milk. More milk."

Ada squinted at her, smiled, threatening discipline, and passed the milk. She watched her daughter and husband eating the same meager dinner she had served them for weeks—hard, dry, monotonous weeks made of too little and too much. Too little rain, too little to eat, too much work, and too much heat. Aesa put food in his mouth and chewed, but his eyes saw some distant place where his thoughts were. She touched his arm to bring him back. "We should go to the store in Henrytown soon," she said.

"Ummm? I have to fix Horatio's left front shoe" was the tired and mindless response of a man who had spent fourteen hours fighting a plow under the sun.

"There's not much money, but we have plenty to trade," said Ada.

"I have things to trade, too," said Sarah with a goat's milk mustache.

"Does that mean that you must come, too?" her mother teased.

"Yes, that is what it means," she said.

ᔕ ᔕ ᔕ

In the near dark before the sun rose they prepared for the trip to Henrytown. Horatio stood in the yard near the yellow glow of the lantern while Aesa fixed his loose iron shoe. Sarah stroked his silky muzzle and inhaled his scent and the odor of the early morning sage. She helped stretch the harness out across his back, fasten the large buckles, and hitch him to the wagon. He was a fine horse, and huge, and nearly elegant, even though he was attached to an awkward old wagon with high iron wheels.

In the darkness of the shed Ada milked Martha the goat and watched Sarah's silhouette coming toward her against the dim morning light. Just outside the shed a cat sat with kittens in a line, intent on the white streamers of milk that shot from goat to bucket. Sarah crouched down across from her mother and began milking. The cat and kittens watched and waited. A stream of milk shot out from the darkness of the shed. The milk-wet cats licked themselves and purred. Sarah pressed her head into Martha's soft warm flank and smiled.

A box of hinges, latches, and knives from Aesa's forge, a rug from Ada's loom, and four baskets of grain were loaded into the wagon. Sarah brought her own box of treasures. It was made of tin and painted on top with the faces of many animals. She examined the contents as the wagon lurched over the ruts in the road: clay marbles and glass ones with swirls, seashells, a round red stone, a square of fancy embroidery with an unusual antelope, a long braid made of hair from Horatio's mane, a rattlesnake's rattle, a dried-up toad, and a long yellow sash.

As the sun came up behind them they crossed the high plain on a road that was nothing more than wagon ruts. They traveled several miles over a sage-covered prairie, through woods, and then across a creek that ran through the bottomland. Here their road of ruts met another with deeper, wider ruts—the main road to Henrytown.

They passed a family of eight, walking single file along the side of the road. Sarah waved to them but they did not wave back. Heads bowed, they saw feet and little else, nor did they speak when Aesa offered them a ride.

Near Henrytown Sarah saw a strange sight in a field near the road. A man, a woman, and three children had erected several unusual machines: a long trumpet-drum on a tripod, a short, fat trumpet-drum on the ground, and a large fan made of a wood propeller covered with copper sheeting, beneath which burned a smoky pile of burlap bags. One of the children turned the fan with a hand crank while another tossed a fine red powder into the rising smoke. The third child was standing on the wagon, jumping and shrieking with delight. The entire family had a reddish hue. Several people stood along the road in the thin shade of the dying trees and stared at the sky and the thin clouds.

Sarah pointed to the reddish family. "What are they doing?" she asked.

"I think they're trying to make it rain," said her mother.

Three stern men on fat horses watched the pro-
ceedings from the side of the road. They were
perched on saddles made of woven wicker. Many
small mirrors were sewn onto their jackets and along
the sides of their britches.

Sarah tugged at her mother. "Look. Who are they?"

"Watchers, watching," said Ada.

The drums began beating at the sky and red smoke
billowed up toward the thin, drifting clouds. "It clouds
some, but never rains," said Aesa, bringing Horatio to
a stop. "That man's a dreamraker, but if he's lucky, his
luck'll be ours. So cast these folks a little wheat."

They took a few grains of wheat from one of the
baskets and flung them toward the dust-red family.

"Good luck," Sarah whispered, then she turned
and whispered in her mother's ear, "What's a dreamraker?"

Ada smiled and said, "Someone who can't make
your dreams real, so he sells you your worst fears."

Sarah studied the hopeful faces along the road.
"They paid?" she asked.

"Yes. They're afraid it won't rain, so they pay the
rainmaker. He beats on the clouds and blows smoke at
the sky, but he knows that won't make it rain."

Sarah looked up at the wispy clouds. "And after he
leaves and the rain doesn't come, they'll still be afraid,
won't they?"

"Yes," said Ada with a glint in her eye, "so he's sold them what they had to begin with."

Sarah climbed down from the wagon and walked to the rainmakers. She studied each of them and their machines. The man twitched and one eyelid fluttered. The woman brooded. The children were dutiful, observant, and dirty, except the smallest. She was elated and dirty.

Their machines were fanciful constructions of wood and copper, painted with arabesque designs and figures of deer, birds, fish, rainbows, and a man, a woman, and three children who operated elaborate machines made of wood and copper. These machines were painted, in turn, with the same wonderful designs and very small figures of deer, birds, fish, rainbows, and tiny people operating tiny machines.

Sarah returned to the wagon, climbed up, and stood between Aesa and Ada. She used her hands to demonstrate the size of the pictures as she described them: "They have pictures on their wagons with pictures of the pictures on the pictures, with the same pictures inside them, only tiny." She held her fingers to show how tiny the tiny pictures were.

"But will it rain?" her father asked.

"I don't know that," she said.

3

GIRKINCOD

၍ ၍ ၍

Henrytown hid in the woods, more an encamp-ment than a town. Shacks and garden patches and wary inhabitants lurked among the trees. Slow, sturdy folks with long looks glared, grunted, or snorted their disapproval. Many had a strange, though barely noticeable, pale cast to their skin. Sarah held her mother's hand and watched.

Aesa pulled Horatio up alongside a mud-brick building as Sarah read the gray, weathered sign and guessed at what it meant to say: "Bracken's Goods and . . ."

And what? she wondered.

A window of glass slabs two inches thick and placed in rows was set deep in the thick mud wall. Men sat in front on barrels. They chewed mundungus. They watched. They had nothing to say and neither spoke nor nodded when Aesa looked their way.

Sarah followed her mother and father up the steps to the store but stopped short when she heard someone shouting. Down the street several children her age and older dragged a small animal through the dirt with a rope, hitting it with sticks and shouting a chant:

Hairyweed tibbletodd
Hoosta goosta
Girkincod.

She ran down the steps and into the street toward the children and shouted, "Stop it! Stop! You'll kill it."

They stopped in their tracks and looked at her. A small, dirty child shouted back: "It's dead, stupid. We already killed it."

The animal lay still in the dust. The children stared at Sarah, not knowing what to make of her.

She walked up to the animal and crouched beside it. But it was not dead, only knocked senseless. It opened an eye and blinked. Sarah slipped the rope off its head and patted it.

Far down the street, hunched and pinched like a cold wet dog, a nervous woman in a lizard-skin turban kept an eye on her. The Lizard Woman gave a startled jump when she saw the fox come alive at Sarah's touch. It struggled to its feet, then bound past the children and disappeared between two ramshackle buildings.

The children gave chase, leaving Sarah alone in the street, but the little fox had made his escape. Sarah watched them go, then turned and crossed the street to the store.

Ada stood in the doorway, waiting. "That was very brave," she said.

"It was a fox, Mother." Sarah looked at her hand and smiled. "I touched it, too."

Down the street the Lizard Woman waved her arms and turned in a circle. She stopped for a moment and stood, staring toward the store. Her head shook slightly. She trembled and put three fingers together with a fourth and made a sign to ward away the evil she had just seen. She was certain that, with only a touch, the child had brought a dead fox to life. An unnatural thing.

ᔕ ᔕ ᔕ

Five men and a pretty woman with tired eyes sat or stood about in the store. They did not appear to be buying anything. They waited and watched.

The Lizard Woman eased the door open and peered in. Her dark, deep-set eyes searched for the strange child who had resurrected the dead fox. But Sarah was on the other side of the store hidden behind several sacks of grain. She was standing on a floor scale weighing herself and whatever else was at hand. The woman edged across the store until she was standing in front of the windows. She spotted Sarah, whose attention was now fixed on a collection of hideous masks made of animal skins, feathers, beaks, claws, stones, and cloth on flat, thin pieces of wood attached to sticks for holding. The child held up a mask that had flat black stones for eyes, a long sharp beak, and blue feathers.

The Lizard Woman was transfixed. She stared, silhouetted against the boom of window light.

Sarah put the mask to her face and slowly turned in a circle, examining the store through the tiny holes drilled in the flat black eyes.

"Child!" someone shouted. She turned toward the shout and through the tiny eyeholes she could see Bracken shaking a finger at her. "Not toys, child. Not for play," he said in a stern, heavy voice.

"I didn't know," she said, a little embarrassed, and set the mask down. She stood very still and watched.

The trading between Aesa and Bracken was done in gestures and few words. Aesa's hinges were refused. The latches and knives were taken. Each transaction moved them farther down the long counter, leaving their past deals and dealings behind them: goods set against goods, better than an account book, for the accumulation gave each man a guide for the next deal.

As they moved down the counter each trade took longer, for the trade in progress was based on all the others. Everything had to be reconsidered each and every time. So it was a single trade—a continuous progression of transactions, reconsiderations, and adjustments.

Sarah studied this elongated trade. She squinched the space between her eyebrows and watched the ebb and flow of dealings between her father and the strange man with pointed eyebrows and hairy ears.

Aesa enjoyed this trading game and in his own farmer way was as cagey as Bracken, whose sly humor slid off his quick proprietor's tongue and whose quick, haggard eyes betrayed his anxious life.

"No new buildings," Bracken said. "No one comes. No rain. People go away."

"Yes," said Aesa. He dug a thin, ruby-colored stone from a small leather pouch and with it obtained a file and a hoop of thick wire to make nails.

"Surprised you've managed to survive in this drought, Aesa. Tell me your secret," said Bracken.

"I could use some work." Aesa's big teeth grinned at Bracken. "Who would need a smith?"

"Hmmm? I might know a 'who would.' For ten hours pay I'll send him to you. Acceptable?"

"Three hours." Aesa bartered back. "And only if there's more than a day's work."

"I'll consider," said Bracken.

Ada came up to the counter and set down sacks of salt and sugar. "I'll need flour, too. Would you trade us twenty-five pounds of flour for fifty of grain?"

"Twenty's the best I'll do," said Bracken.

"You're a little desperate today, Mr. Bracken."

Bracken looked at her with a slight, thin smile. "You know you've got two neighbors who've lost their wells—Silas and the Hardkeel woman. She's left the valley and you'll be next." He raised his eyebrows. "We're all desperate," he said.

An old man, who had been listening, came over, wheezing and short of breath. He leaned toward Aesa. "It's a curse," said the wheezing man. "That's what they say: It's a curse. All the other valleys, they got rain— north and south. It's only us that's dry. What d'you make a' that, meestar?"

Aesa pulled away from him and followed Ada and Bracken toward the back of the building to sack up some overpriced flour.

Sarah's attention had been captured by the woman in the lizard-skin turban who muttered magic rhymes, whose hands darted across her body making signs to ward off evil things. Sarah's stare unnerved the woman.

The Lizard Woman gnawed at her hand. "The child knows," she said to herself. "She can see into me. She must know."

Fear burned in her mind. Her face glistened with sweat. She knew the child could see deep into her soul. Indeed, her secret was impressed in each line and crevice of her flesh—in her walk, in her dark, dead eyes, in the strangled way she arched her shoulders toward her long, skinny neck. She could feel something inside herself dissolve, then evaporate up into the rafters of the dismal store.

Something cold and wet uncoiled in her brain. Her head seemed to slip from her neck. She reached out, grabbing the air, but fell back in a stone-dead faint amid sacks of chickpeas, shriveled tubers, and moldy corn.

Several people moved toward her. The pretty woman with tired eyes waved spirits under the Lizard Woman's nose. She woke gasping, arms raised to ward off unseen evils, the turban still fast to her head.

"The child's a fiend," she whispered to the crowd. "She's taken over by evil."

Their faces twitched. Their wide eyes darted back and forth to catch each other's fear.

Sarah studied their backs. Slowly their heads pivoted around so they could watch from the corners of their eyes. Sarah smiled at them. They looked back at the Lizard Woman, confused, not ready to believe her accusation.

Sarah was puzzled. She began to walk toward the distraught woman. The woman whimpered. She knew that the child had only to touch her and her soul would turn into a small black brick that smelled of ferret dung.

Aesa came from the back of the store and told Sarah to wait outside. The storekeeper's attitude had changed from sullen appraisal to apprehension. He did not argue with the girl's parents, wanting only that they should leave, taking their troublesome child as they went.

Outside, Sarah looked up and down the street. She stood next to Horatio and patted his nose. She turned and looked back at the store. Several distorted faces peered through the window glass. Each face examined her through its own prism of evils.

She studied their faces: amusing, horrible, and wondrous faces trapped in fat glass. They became more menacing than strange, and she turned away.

She took a willow stick from the wagon and began to draw a large skritchy picture in the road. She was absorbed and unaware of the Lizard Woman, who came out of the store holding one of Bracken's masks to her face. The woman walked away in a hurried, stiff-legged gait. Sarah drew in the dirt.

Aesa and Ada carried their sacks and bundles from the store and loaded them in the wagon. "You didn't trade anything?" Ada said to her daughter.

"Didn't want anything," said Sarah.

Far down the street the Lizard Woman spoke with rapid gestures to the three men of many mirrors on wide horses. The people of Henrytown called them the Triune. They paid close attention to her. One of them wrote down every word.

The Lizard Woman fell silent. She held the strange animal mask to her face and peered through the tiny eyeholes at Sarah and her parents until they drove away.

§ § §

Near the edge of town Sarah saw a small crowd gathered before a robust man who stood in the back of a high-sided wagon. He held a translucent block above his head with one hand. With his free hand he pointed to the distant mountains. His words were slow and round:

Miraculous ice from mount'n caves.
Miraculous ice from mount'n caves.

The robust man moved with large, stiff gestures—a stuffed toy come to life. His eyes were bright and his cheeks glowed. He was obviously not from Henrytown, and it was possible that the ice business was also new to him. He would look at a customer, look at the block of ice that had the customer's interest, gauge the customer

again, and slowly name a price, his voice rising to a
question mark, leaving the entire matter in doubt and
open to negotiation. It was as though he had, at that
very moment, invented the selling of ice.

Sarah scrambled from the wagon before it stopped,
and threaded her way through the crowd until she was
standing before the robust man's sawdust-caked boots.
Behind him a mound of sawdust protected his ice from
the sun's heat. His plump red hands pawed the sawdust
for another block—one about a foot square and five
inches thick. He carefully brushed the ice clean and
offered it to the crowd, "Miraculous ice from mount'n
caves."

A man waved and asked, "Will this ice cure fever?"

"This ice," he said in his slow, rolling way, "will ease
a fever and soothe a burning throat. Crush this ice
with a hard rock, pour over it redberry wine. You will
have a delight—a miraculous concoction. If it fails to
cure, you may at least endure the suffering." The
robust man laughed, but his laughter was not taken up
by the crowd.

"What's miraculous about this ice, anyway?" asked a
hostile man with a bear's voice.

"When did you last see ice, my friends?" They were
silent, as it had been a very long time—some had never
seen ice, miraculous or otherwise. "Well then, isn't it
miraculous that in this heat we have ice at all? That is

certainly a miracle," and laughter rolled from him.

"But I believe that this ice is the most beautiful ice I have ever seen." His words were slow and careful. "It is clean and clear. Have you ever seen ice so pure?" He smiled at his ice and held it out to them. And indeed, it was clean and clear; free of bubbles, flaws, or specks of dirt; made of water distilled by the far distant mountains and frozen for hundreds, perhaps thousands, of years. It glistened in his hands.

"May I see, please?"

The robust man looked down upon the brightest face he had ever seen.

Sarah liked the robust man and was thrilled at the prospect of ice, which she had only heard of, but never touched. She grinned at him. He stooped down and offered her the block of ice. She looked deep into the ice, then looked at the robust man and laughed. What a strange thing for water to be, she thought, and reached out to touch it.

She yelped in surprise and jumped. "It's hot!"

"Just the opposite, it's cold," he said.

She pressed her fingers to her lips to feel the cold. She laughed again. The robust man beamed. "Take this ice. This ice is for you."

"All of it?"

"Of course. Take all of it." He laughed, climbed down, and made his way through the crowd, carrying the ice above his head. Sarah followed close behind. He looked up at Ada and Aesa and said, "I believe she has some secret power over me. I am giving my precious ice away." He set the ice in a corner of the wagon and began piling straw around it. "To help it keep," he said.

Sarah stood in the wagon and held out her closed hand with a gift for the robust man. He put his opened hand out to her and she placed her precious red stone in it.

"Very beautiful," he said, and smiled.

As they were about to leave there was a scuffle in the crowd around the ice wagon. One man shoved a larger one who in turn punched him with a terrible blow to the side of his head. He fell hard against the ground and lay quiet and still, either unconscious, afraid to move, or dead. The large man bent over him, breathing hard, waiting, ready to strike.

The shock of this made Sarah cry out. She felt the terrible force of the blow and put her hands to her temples. The crowd turned its gaze on her. The large man, fists clenched, looked up. He had one milk-white eye and one blue.

Aesa popped Horatio's reins and they were away. The pale-skinned crowd stared after them. Sarah stared back. The robust man, confused and saddened by the fight, watched them go. Only when they were gone did he think to wave, so he waved to the faraway mountains and the high and wispy distant clouds.

§ § §

The Lizard Woman, the three horsemen of the Triune, and five children studied Sarah's drawing in the road in front of Bracken's store. Their interest attracted several others to puzzle over the mystery made by the strange child.

The Triune's purpose was to maintain order, devise punishments, investigate wrongdoing. They satisfied the want for order and pleased the councilmen of Henrytown. The man in charge was Kreel, who had a face like an ax. And there was Greyling Eyes, who was nimble and nasty, and Henkel, Keeper of Records, who was round.

They rode in saddles made of wicker. Their horses were fat. The Keeper of Records commanded a small wicker desk woven to his saddle and leather bags with books protruding.

The man in charge gave orders to the Keeper of Records, who wrote small, careful words in a large ledger on his precarious perch. Though the writing was difficult and ink often splattered about, Henkel drew well and was able to copy exactly the mystery drawn in dirt. Once reduced to the ledger page it became clear that the child had drawn an animal. Indeed, it was a fox.

Henkel held his ledger so the Lizard Woman could see. Tiny sparks jumped around in her brain. She fished in her big leather bag and came out with a bottle of dark purple powder. This she sprinkled on the drawing at her feet. She chanted, "naa naa-naa, naa naa-naa" over and over, and began stamping the ground—stamping out the drawing by the demon child. The children liked the chant and liked to stamp. They joined the Lizard Woman and soon a cloud of dust rose up out of the street and above the town.

The crowd at the ice wagon near the edge of town, alerted by the chanting children, began moving toward the rising plume of dust.

The robust man watched them go. A slight smile brightened his face. He had lost his enthusiasm for selling ice in this place. Now he was free of them, free of sour looks, suspicious eyes, and hostile voices. "Well," he said to his team of snow-white mares, "they're ripe to get drummed up about most anything. Could've been us, ladies." He made a chick-chick sound in his cheek and they turned into the road and headed down the valley in search of greener pastures and people not so mean.

4

A LIZARD
ON WHEELS

🌀 🌀 🌀

Sarah pushed the straw back and slid her fingers over the beautiful ice as the wagon creaked its way along the path through the sagebrush.

Aesa turned to watch her. "Sarah, break us off a piece of your ice." He reached under the seat, pulled a hammer from his tool box, and handed it down to her. He turned his attention back to Horatio and the sagebrush, waiting to hear the sound of ice breaking.

She grasped the hammer in both hands and looked at her perfect ice. She wanted to keep it just as it was. Perfect, clear, and ancient ice. Her father looked at her. Her mother, too.

She raised the hammer above her head, shut her eyes, and brought the hammer down hard. The sound of ice breaking in a hot prairie in a drought surprised Ada and made her smile.

The small chunks slipped through Sarah's fingers and skittered away. She caught them in the cup of her hand and offered them to her mother and father.

She held a piece of the precious ice, letting the melt drip through her fingers onto the little animal faces painted on the hot tin top of her treasure box. Steam rose from the little faces. She opened her hand and examined the ice. She put it in her mouth and sucked, making a face without lips, and watched the prairie slide by. The sun was high and the prairie was hot.

"Mother?"

"Hmm?"

"What were the funny animal faces for?"

"What animal faces?"

"Ones on sticks," said Sarah.

"People hold them to their faces when something evil comes, so the evil can't see into them."

"Why didn't we buy some?"

"They're not needed," said Ada.

"Bracken's a dreamraker, isn't he?"

"Yes," Ada laughed. "A dreamraker."

After Redberry Canyon, after Beetle Bluff, and after old, white horse bones hidden under sagebrush, they saw, far off in the distant prairie, a dark figure. Perhaps the heatwaves made it seem so strange, for the top part appeared to have a head and a long, thick neck, but the bottom part seemed to have wheels.

As Sarah watched, her curiosity grew. She could not make out just what it was she was seeing, because it kept changing its shape. At times it looked like a burro; other times it looked something like a lizard. Then it disappeared into a gully, but a little later it floated up the other side and continued on its way. The mystified child looked at her parents and wondered if they knew what she did not. She watched them watching, but did not ask. It was a mystery now. A mystery should last.

What Ada knew was that the strange figure was on another road that would join the one they were on and soon enough they would know who or what it was that played such tricks on their eyes.

Aesa noticed the strangeness in the distance, but was deep in other thoughts. He watched the dry stubble between the ruts of the road as it rolled under the wagon. He studied the curled black leaves of trees, the dry spring bed, and a horse, not long dead, in a gully. He could feel something new and different about the drought, but fear had a claw in his brain and he could not find words for his feelings. Then something flashed by his face and startled him. He turned and saw a small red bird with yellow eyes and a sharp black beak hovering above the wagon.

"It can smell the ice," said Ada.

The bird turned and flew away. In the distance it caught a current in the sky, flew up, and vanished out of sight.

Aesa's thoughts came back to the drought and he realized what was new and different—he had stopped waiting for rain. Rain was no longer a possibility to him. He only wondered where he would take his family. How would they survive?

"What will I do?" he said aloud, startled by his own voice. Ada looked at him. She touched his arm to reassure him, for she knew what was in his mind.

Sarah was much too fascinated by the strange figure moving through the heatwaves on the other road to hear her father's words. She realized that what she had been watching was not a black lizard on wheels, but a stooped and ancient woman dressed in black from head to toe, pulling a small cart loaded with belongings.

Ada noticed there was something familiar in the old woman's walk and in the stoop of her shoulders. "Aesa. Aesa, look—that woman."

He pulled Horatio to a stop where the roads met and watched the old woman approach. He watched in disbelief. The old woman was oblivious. She kept her eyes to the road and continued on until she was even with Horatio, then turned, and started down the road ahead of them.

Aesa called to her, "Hello?"

The old woman stopped, turned, and looked back in the direction of the voice. She squinted, then slowly pulled her stiff and gnarled hands loose from the cart handles and walked back toward the wagon. She shaded the sun from her eyes and peered up at Aesa.

A tiny, tired voice came from her dry throat, cracking her words: "I'm your Grandmother Lilly. Don't you recognize your own grandmother?"

Aesa stared down at his ancient grandmother, at her overloaded cart and her old rotted shoes. "What's happened, Grandmother? Have you come to live with us?"

She stared at the sky. "It rained hard for too long. We were washed away. The town . . . the town washed away." She squinted back down the road, then up at the sun, and finally into Aesa's eyes. "I've come to live with you. What do you think of it?"

He smiled. "I think it would be good, Grandmother."

"And I think so as well," said Ada, for she felt considerable affection for the old woman.

Lilly made a smile that to a stranger would be a grimace. She looked up at Sarah in the wagon and asked, "Who are you, child?"

"My name is Sarah, and that's Horatio." The horse, hearing his name, twitched his ears, and turned to see.

"You may call me Lilly, Sarah. I am your great-grandmother. It is my good luck to meet you—and your very strong horse." She paused, trying to remember why the horse was so important to her. Then she looked up at her grandson. "Aesa, may I ride in the wagon? I'm tired. It is so hot and dry."

Aesa lifted her into the wagon and Ada gave her the waterskin and some bread and cheese. They loaded her belongings and the cart while she ate. Sarah's eyes were fixed on the old woman's strange hands, twisted, gnarled hands, with lumps and blotches on the lumps.

The hungry grandmother—the dark, rapacious mouse-beast—attacked her bread and cheese. Then she paused, having noticed that she was closely watched. She restrained her attack and slowly, somewhat timidly, looked up. Sarah smiled at her. Lilly grinned back. "I saw you before, you know. You were like this," she said, spreading her hands to show a baby's length, "and pink." She dropped her bread and Sarah picked it up for her. The old woman took the bread, clutched it, and giggled. Sarah thought that Lilly was very different, but in a way she liked.

She turned so Lilly could not see and broke off a small piece of the no longer perfect ice. She turned back to her great-grandmother and smiled her sly smile. "Close your eyes," she said.

"Why should I close my eyes?"

"Surprise."

"Surprise?"

"Something hot and cold at the same time."

Lilly resigned herself to the torture of "surprise," closed her eyes, and put out her hands. Sarah dropped the ice into the waiting hands. Lilly felt the ice. She rubbed it between her hands and brought it to her cheek, her eyes still closed. "Ice," she said in disbelief. "Ice," as though it were a distant memory. She put the ice in her mouth, and without opening her eyes, lay down and fell deep asleep.

She appeared to have walked for miles and for days. Neither the heat nor the jostling wagon could wake her. Sarah sat next to her and watched her sleep. Around Lilly's neck was a necklace made of many dark red stones. Sarah touched them, one by one, and Lilly slept.

They came to a fork in the road and stopped. Aesa looked down the road to the west. "We should visit Silas, even if he is a little mean and crazy."

"He likes Horatio fine," said Ada. "Let the horse visit him."

Sarah rolled her eyes. Lilly slept and the sun sank low in the sky.

The road to Silas's took them through a land of red ravines and pale green sandstone cliffs worn deep by ancient rivers. Thick blue lizards and glossy black stones hid beneath the dry sagebrush.

The shadows of Sarah and her parents, high-iron-wheeled and drawn by the huge Horatio, slid, long and narrow over the prairie, up boulders and down, over sagebrush, and across the face of the pale green cliffs.

Lilly did not stir. She slept in a small curl and dreamed. She dreamed there was a pool of fresh water hidden in a ravine. Its presence was made known by shocks of emerald green grass along its edge. Aesa, Ada, and Sarah laughed and splashed and swam in the clear, cool pool. Their waves surged toward the bank and washed through the emerald grass. Along the edge a long thick snake, mottled green and black, moved her perfect head back and forth, and with a quick red tongue sampled the cool air for the smell of them. She slipped into the pond and slid over the water behind their splash and frolic. They were unaware of the snake; unaware even that they had nothing to fear from this creature, who was sweet, and serene, and merely indifferent to them—a peaceful snake in an old woman's dream.

§ § §

They drove on, crossing a hump in the benchland, seeing in the distance a small, black shack and a shed that undulated and twisted in the hot air rising, perhaps escaping, from the dry earth, even though the sun was low in the sky. Behind them a distant plume of smoke rose from the edge of the southern horizon. It turned from black to gray and disappeared.

They stopped in front of the shack. Everyone was still, even Horatio, listening in the heat for signs of life. Then they heard the sound of water dripping. They held their breath and listened, except for Lilly, who slept. Horatio's ears twitched, searching for the dripping water, then he turned his head and looked back at the wagon.

"The ice," Sarah whispered. "The ice is melting." She leaned over the sideboard and watched drops of icewater splatter on the hard red earth.

Aesa climbed down and walked to the door of the shack, knocked, waited, then called out. The head of an animal, its swirl of horns intact and its skin in tatters, hung above the door, a warning to trespassers and thieves. Aesa walked around to the back of the shack.

Small chickens of many colors pecked at the bare ground. A she-goat with twisted horns watched from the shed.

Next to Silas's well was a high mound of dirt and rock. He had evidently been digging his well deeper.

Aesa looked out across the field, then walked to the shed and peered in. He went to the corral and patted Silas's old white horse. "Where is Silas?" he asked the horse, who pushed his muzzle against Aesa's chest, not for affection, but for water.

Sarah discovered a strange and twisted shape in the dried mud near the well. She poked it with her foot and uncovered a torn burlap sack and a piece of rope. She tugged at the sack. It fell apart in her hands, rotted and dry.

Ada sat at the well, waiting. She turned, masking the sun from her eyes, and peered down into the dark well. Gradually a shape appeared in the darkness below. It was rather round and white. And then she realized it was the top of Silas's head. The earth had caved in and killed him. Her cry for Aesa rang and echoed from the well.

Sarah started for her mother, but Ada's look stopped her. "You don't need to see this, Sarah."

"But I want to see. What is it?"

Aesa crossed the yard in giant strides. He leaned over the low wall and studied the darkness below. He looked up at his daughter: "It's Silas. He's dead, Sarah. He was digging his well deeper and it caved in on him."

She was quiet for a moment, her eyes large, and her heart fast. She had to see. "I've never seen a dead person."

Aesa and Ada looked at her then to each other.

"I have to sometime," she said.

Ada looked down at the dim shape of the dead Silas and then back to her daughter. "If you are sure, Sarah."

Timid and curious, Sarah peered into the well. Her eyes were wide. Her breathing stopped. After a moment she was able to make out the whiteness that was Silas's head. She remembered the stiff, coarse, white hair that seemed to shoot out from his head. His hair was just like him. He was like a porcupine, she thought, a white porcupine. And now he was dead and there was his hair, glowing at her in the darkness of the well.

Her father's voice broke through her thoughts: "Sarah, I want you to let Silas's horse out. We can't afford to keep him. Then catch his chickens and tie the goat to our wagon."

Aesa grabbed the windlass rope and eased himself down into the well. He scooped dirt and rock from around Silas's head with the bucket, and Ada pulled the bucket up, emptied it, and lowered it again to Aesa.

Sarah wrestled with the high corral gate and finally managed to set the horse free. He put his head up and trotted into the field, then stopped and looked back toward the yard. The old horse and the child stood perfectly still, each one considering the purpose and plan of the other.

Then the horse turned and looked across the

benchland to the south. He stood, fixed in the field, not knowing what to do with his freedom. He watched the last edge of sun slide under the sky, then he turned east, and set off at a serious walk in search of water.

Sarah patted the goat and enticed her with grain to follow her to the wagon. "Come with me and be my goat," she sang. "Silas Goat will be your name."

Ada pulled the bucket up, dumped it, and sent it down again.

Sarah herded the uncooperative, flapping chickens. Bits and pieces of brightly colored feathers flashed in the dust. Yellow, blue, and red. Five chickens and five directions. The chickens squawked.

Digging Silas out was difficult. Aesa had little room in which to work. The wall continued to cave in, and the sun was down, leaving only a dim light to invade the darkness of the well.

One by one Sarah cornered the chickens inside the shed. She pounced, held them in straw until they went soft, then stuffed them in a gunnysack. They were quiet and still and waited for whatever was next.

ဖ ဖ ဖ

There was a whoosh from the well and a plume of dust shot up. Ada screamed and Sarah ran to the well.

Ada shouted for her husband in the rising dust. Then she was quiet. "Aesa," she whispered. But there was no answer.

Sarah squinted into the dust. She realized that what happened to Silas had happened to her father: The wall had caved in on him. She tried to speak, but nothing came. Finally she managed a slow, terrified whisper: "Please, Father."

But the world was dust and silence.

Then the rope quivered. Through the dust a hand reached up and clutched the rope, then another hand, then Aesa's dusty head emerged. He struggled free, looked up with a small smile, and blinked at his wife and daughter. "Yes," was all he could manage.

He climbed out of the well, breathed deeply, and peered back in. "I guess we have just buried our good friend Silas."

Sarah sat on the mound next to the well in the dim light, her arms wrapped around her knees, and rocked back and forth. She said nothing.

Ada brought the head with horns from the house and attached it to the windlass. They stood looking at Silas's resting place for a moment, then Aesa picked Sarah up and pulled Ada close to him. Only their eyes and the outlines of their faces showed in the evening light. They held each other tightly and looked into each other's eyes.

Another face emerged from the dusk. It was Lilly, finally awake and looking for them. She had a story to tell: "I dreamed you found a pool of clear water with green, green grass growing around it. You all went swimming. The most perfect snake swam by. You didn't see it so you never thought to be afraid. It swam by and didn't mind you at all. Isn't that a wonderful dream?"

"A pool of clear water?" Aesa asked her.

"Yes, clear and cool."

"Yes, Grandmother. A wonderful dream."

ෆ ෆ ෆ

They discovered Silas Goat sitting under the wagon, her nose pressed against the bedboards, drinking drops of melting ice.

The moon sailed along telling the clouds, and Sarah and Lilly sat close in the wagon speaking in whispers. The chickens slept in a gunnysack and the tethered goat with a cold nose followed them home.

"What happened when Silas died?" the child asked. "Did he go to sleep forever?"

"His soul went away," the great-grandmother replied.

"Where does a soul go when it goes away?"

"It goes dancing."

"Dancing? True?"

"Yes, dancing," said Lilly.

"Forever?" asked Sarah. But Lilly had fallen asleep and the moon slid through night clouds that had no rain. Sarah sucked on a piece of the ice that would melt before morning and considered the dancing soul of the departed Silas.

5

THE STRANGEST
THING

§ § §

Lilly leaned against the morning sky. Her bent and crooked hands pushed a crooked stick into the deep black loam to make a trail of small poke holes for the child sower of seeds who squatted, walking duck-like behind, to deposit with thumb and forefinger one-at-a-time beans.

"Guess what?" said Sarah. "I found a big stone in the field."

"A big stone in the field?"

"It has writing on it—but my father can't read it."

"Hmmm."

"You could read it. It's very old. It was written by longago people. Come, I'll show you."

Sarah ran halfway to the well, stopped, ran back, and walked beside Lilly, holding her crooked fingers.

At the well Lilly bent forward and peered at the stone. She straightened slightly and pronounced: "I have seen this kind of writing. The Yellow Sailors wrote this way."

"Yellow?"

"Yes."

"Really yellow?"

"Yellow as buttercups. Long ago they came from across the sea. They made beautiful gardens and grew flowers on the hillsides and in the valley."

"Where are they now?"

"They went away," said Lilly. Her voice trailed off, following a memory.

"Away where?"

"Far away . . . the high mountains where no one goes."

"Why?"

Lilly stared at the distant peaks. The tone of her voice changed. She was still speaking to a child, but to a child in her distant past, to herself, perhaps: "They are such beautiful flowers. In the summer you can see them on the high peaks . . . many tiny white flowers."

Sarah peered up at her, amazed, then looked across the benchland toward the far distant mountains with their white peaks.

Lilly did not move. She stood and stared and hummed a tune. Sarah waited, trying to make sense of

Lilly. Finally she asked, "Why would they put writing on a stone?"

Lilly stopped her humming and looked at the slate-with-words. She became her old self. "It must be a gravestone. There must be a Yellow Sailor buried in the field."

"We better put it back then. Right?"

"Yes, maybe. When your father has time." And then, as though to confirm her faith in the future, she said, "Let's put some water on our beans."

ᕼ ᕼ ᕼ

Aesa pumped the giant bellows of his forge to heat an iron bar. The black iron turned dark red in the hot blast. Then the red began to glow. It turned orange, then light yellow, almost white. He pulled it from the fire with tongs and set it glowing on the anvil. His hammer sent long, ringing, anvil sounds across the yard to Sarah, who drew water from the well. The ringing filled the sky and echoed on the hills.

She turned the windlass round and round until the bucket was high enough to grab with the hook. She pulled the bucket to the wall, balanced it to pour, and filled her garden pail. Then she unreeled the windlass, sending the bucket to the bottom.

As the rope went slack she remembered to check the

mark on the rope against the point where it touched the mark on the windlass. She turned the windlass back until the bucket was lifted out of the water. Then she climbed up onto the wall to see the reflected sky below. She lowered the bucket again until it just touched the patch of bright blue light. She checked the point where the marks on the rope and the windlass met, then she turned to go. But she could not move. Her shoulders were turned away but her eyes were fixed on the rope. Its mark did not touch the windlass mark.

Her heart pounded and all her thoughts stopped, but one. She looked hard at the marks on the rope and the windlass. She turned the windlass back until the two marks met, then she leaned over the well and peered down. The bucket swung free, a dark pendulum above the patch of sky. Only one thought—the well is going dry.

The ringing of the anvil ceased. Aesa called to Sarah for a pail of water to quench the hot iron. But she did not hear him for the ringing in her ears and the pounding in her heart. She let the bucket drop, blurring the blue light. Again Aesa shouted for water. This time she heard.

Small, dry gusts of wind began to sweep through the yard. They pushed her along toward the shed, to the large sweating man and his resounding hammer.

She stood close to him, her hands covering her ears against the anvil's ring and watched him work the radiant blade. He stopped, examined the blade against the light, and plunged it into the cold water. It hissed and spit like an angry snake.

"Why can't we get water from the creek below the cliffs?" she asked above the hissing blade.

"It doesn't belong to us. It's Haggen's water. We'd be trespassing."

"There's a lot of water in the creek," she argued. "They don't need it all. What if we needed drinking water?"

He was hammering again and irritated. Between blows he said, "It's their water. . . . They're not the . . . kind that shares. . . . They're the kind . . . that kills."

"But if the well . . ."

He shouted above the hammering: "Our well's deep. Deeper'n Silas's. . . . It will not . . . dry up."

"But it . . ."

He shouted: "I don't want . . . t'hear another . . . word about it. . . . Understand?"

His shouts carried with the rhythm of the ringing across the yard and above the rising wind to Ada and Lilly in the garden. They looked up to see Sarah run from the shed.

She stopped at the well and hid her head in her arms. Her body shook. After a moment she rubbed the tears from her eyes and looked back toward the shed. Her eyes shifted from her father to her mother and Lilly in the garden to Horatio in the corral.

Ada crossed the yard from the garden and knelt beside her. "What's wrong, Sarah? What happened?"

"Nothing," she said.

The dry, anxious wind blew dirt in their eyes. Ada held her daughter and tried, without success, to shield her from the stinging sand. They ran to the house, followed by Aesa and Lilly.

Sarah stood looking out through the window. What was once only a thought now had the feel of fear around it. "What's gone before is done with," she said to herself. "Something new will happen now." Through the dim light and swirl of dust she watched the wind-blown junipers that hid the mesa from the house.

Her father called her and she turned to him. "I shouldn't have yelled, Sarah. I'm sorry. Is it all right?"

"Yes, it's all right," she said to reassure him for she knew that in some way all of this would be worse for him than for her.

"You must forget the creek, though. People get killed over water. You understand, don't you?"

"Yes," she said, and turned back to watch the wind in the junipers that looked out over the forbidden creek.

Aesa smiled. He assumed he had convinced his stubborn daughter and went out into the subsiding wind to hammer out his knives, and locks, and worries.

Sarah walked through the sage below the house and disappeared into the junipers. She emerged on the mesa above the cliffs and stood looking down on the creek that meandered through the narrow valley. Far upstream, beyond Haggen's land, she could see the sharp reflections of light at the bends in the creek. More than anything she wanted the water to change its course and wind its way up through the cliffs to the benchland and her family's farm. She imagined small fingers of water spreading out in rivulets, running through the dry furrows, and seeping into the dark earth.

It felt mean-minded and very wrong that she could not go down to the creek, even for drinking water. How, she wondered, could Haggen own the water? She remembered the underground river that flowed through their well and guessed it must eventually find its way down to the creek. Certainly her family had as much right to the water as Haggen did.

For a brief moment the bright reflections on the creek seemed to change their shape as though the pull of her desire had altered the water's course. Then the wind blew across the mesa. Dust and topsoil stung her eyes. The ring of her father's anvil caught in the wind, became a song, was carried away and lost.

෨ ෨ ෨

In the distance a man on a horse rose up out of the benchland. Aesa hammered and turned the hot iron and from time to time looked up to measure the rider's progress. The way the man rode, handled his horse, sat in his saddle—such things were like a signature.

Aesa studied the stranger as he rode by the garden and into the yard. His sense of the man was that he was both strong and thoughtful. And then, as though it were as plain as sky, he realized that the man had come to offer him work.

From below the house, coming out of the juniper grove, Sarah saw her father and the stranger talking. The stranger dismounted and followed Aesa toward the house.

Sarah climbed the slope and stood outside the house looking in through the thick glass. Her parents and the stranger sat at the table. Lilly bent over the stove stirring a large soup.

". . . Then the brown mare kicked the poor man," the stranger said and tapped his temple, "right in his blocky head. He's asleep as dead 'n' now we're both a cook 'n' a smith in need."

Lilly, still stirring, not bothering to turn, said, "Sarah and I will be fine. Go if you need."

Aesa watched his grandmother's hunched shoulders

and considered his plight. The possibility of work that paid was shining in his mind. He looked at his wife: "We could be gone for a few days at a time."

"Yes, we should do it," Ada agreed. She could see her daughter against the glass looking in, guessing at the stranger's purpose.

After money talk and weather talk and strong black tea, they gathered in the yard and waved the man good-bye. Sarah hung back, watching from the side of the house. When the man had gone she walked across the yard to her father. "Are you and mother going away?" she asked him.

"Yes, several miles south, to work on a farm."

"Why?"

"So we can eat."

"Am I going to stay with Great-grandmother Lilly?"

"You'll have to do the chores and milk the goats by yourself. Can you do that?"

"Yes, of course," she said. "Can we put the slate-with-words back where it was in the field?"

"Why do that?" asked her mystified father.

"Great-grandmother Lilly said it's the gravestone of a Yellow Sailor that was buried there long, long ago."

He looked at Lilly. "A Yellow Sailor, Grandmother?"

"Yes, Grandson," she said, "a Yellow Sailor," and smiled.

In the late afternoon, Sarah, Lilly, and Ada followed

Aesa up into the field to replace the slate-with-words and to plant the new ground. They stood the slate upright in the dirt at the very edge of the field and braced it with stones against the wind. Then Lilly and Ada and Sarah scooped handfuls of seed from the sack slung over Aesa's shoulder and filled the folds they made in their skirts.

Staggered along the crest of benchland, silhouetted against red streamers of evening sky, they cast seeds in arcs: step and cast, step and cast, step and hope.

And as they cast the last of their seeds, the ball of yellow sun pressed against the blue mountains.

§ § §

In the dim morning light Sarah saw the slow-moving shapes of her parents. Their dark forms came toward her, blocking the light. They kissed her and whispered, "Look after your great-grandmother, feed the chickens, gather the eggs, milk the goats, we love you."

She nodded and through half-opened eyes watched them leave. Then she closed her eyes and floated between dreaming and feeling. She remembered Silas's well, her mother's cry, her father covered with dirt. They held her close between them and looked into each other's eyes. She woke up and went out into the light.

In the shed Sarah scooped two handfuls of grain

into a fold in her yellow nightgown. She walked to the center of the yard and called the chickens from their night roost. They came—yellow, blue, red, and clucking—one, even, from high up on the hill. She spun, scattering grain.

Lilly emerged from the house and waved to her. The old woman walked up the hill and disappeared over the horizon.

Sarah watched, somewhat puzzled. Should she follow? Lilly would come back, of course. She went about her chores: watered the garden and searched for eggs scattered helter-skelter amid sage, rocks, and machinery. Milked the goats. "Where did Great-grandmother go?" she asked the goats. And they played a game called "goats push Sarah until she gives them grain."

Her quest for eggs took her up the hill to where a hen had spent the night. As she reached for an egg near a large flat rock something caught her eye, a small red stone in the dirt at the base of the rock. She scratched the ground for it and discovered others— several red stones, almost round. They were a great find. She clutched them in one hand, the egg in the other, and walked down the hill to the house.

She placed the egg with others in a bowl and put the red stones in a clear glass jar. She held them up to the light, trying to see into their centers. Why would they be all in one place? she wondered.

Sarah walked into the yard and looked up toward the field. The horizon was plain and milky blue. No crooked black figure of an old grandmother.

She climbed up on the edge of the well, grasped the windlass frame with one hand, and leaned over to check the mark on the rope. She rocked the windlass back and forth, moving the bucket up and down to blur the patch of sky at the bottom of the well. The mark on the rope was slightly lower than before. She found another piece of charcoal, made a new mark, and hid the charcoal in the windlass frame. She climbed down and sat on the ground next to the well. And waited.

She studied the horizon. The sun stared down at her, refusing to move. Time floated in the still air. She imagined she saw something small and black like a bird hopping on the crest of the hill. She stood up, and there was Lilly's small, black shape stepping carefully through the sage at the edge of the field. With small one-at-a-time steps she made her way down the hill. Sarah ran to meet her.

As the child approached she saw that the ancient woman clutched something in her hand: a bouquet of small white flowers.

Home and hungry, Lilly ate her breakfast of porridge and black roots. A glass jar in the center of the table held Lilly's small white flowers and Sarah's round red stones.

Sarah watched her eat and Lilly was aware of being watched. She had to undo thirty years of eating alone.

ʃ ʃ ʃ

Heat, flies, dust, and boredom. Sarah waited for her great-grandmother to take her nap. Lilly finally went off to her bed under the loft stairs and curled up. To put herself to sleep she told Sarah a small story: "When I was a young girl, I was sitting in a meadow one day watching the clouds and I just went away to a faraway place. I saw amazing things. I understood the secret of the universe. I thought, I must remember this. And when I came back to the meadow, all I could remember was—I must remember this."

She smiled at Sarah and closed her eyes. Soon her breathing was deep and long and her chest rattled. Sarah leaned close and listened. And then, sure that Lilly was asleep, she took two waterskins from a peg on the wall, tied them together with the yellow sash from her treasure box, and set off toward the mesa.

With the waterskins slung over her shoulders, she descended the deer trail through cliffs that rose like clumsy stalagmites from the hillside, and followed the twisting trail to the canyon floor. It was quiet at first, without the wind. A sharp, nasty cry behind her and above made her jump, but she realized in the same instant that it was only a magpie and she laughed. Her laughter echoed back and forth across the canyon.

Once she reached the bottom she fought her way through a dense cover of thistle, through red thrashberry bushes with their black thorns, and finally yellow tangleweed. She heard dogs in the distance and stopped to listen. The dogs faded away and she heard the strange singing sounds of the creek.

As she made her way through the thistle toward the creek she came upon a peculiar site. Thrashberry thorns had wound themselves around a cluster of tangleweed that clutched a weathered post. The post was held upright by a pile of large stones covered with blood-lichens and stinging moss. Nailed to the post was an old sign, and hidden in its weathered wood were the words NOT THIS WAY. Stuck on top of the post was something bone-white and partially covered with green-black lichens. She climbed the stones for a closer look. It was a skull, too small for a person's, more the size of a large cat, but nothing she knew. She guessed it was from very long ago and whoever put it there was gone away or dead. She stepped down with great care, not wanting to touch a thing so poisonous and mean, and resumed her purpose.

She found the singing creek, stretched out on its bank, and peered over the edge into the water—a fish swam there. She dipped her waterskins into the creek to fill, then started back toward the cliffs. This part seemed so easy, as long as the dogs did not come after her.

She began her climb and very soon the waterskins became heavy. Before long the trail became steep and the dirt was loose. Climbing became work. Hair stuck to her damp forehead, and the waterskins bounced, throwing her off balance. Her feet slipped, the thistles stuck, and burrs grabbed. She came to a steep rock slant and crossed anxiously, arms outstretched to counterbalance the swaying waterskins. Near the top she slipped on small loose stones, fell, and slid off the trail.

She grabbed a thistle stalk to stop her fall. For a moment everything was still. What was to be a wail was stifled to a whimper. Slowly she climbed back onto the trail, stood, and pulled the tiny thistle stickers from her hand with small winces. Sarah looked down the trail, pleased at the progress she'd made, then adjusted the waterskins and prepared to finish the climb.

She looked up to see how far she had to go and there, peering over the mesa ledge, was a fox. It looked directly at her for a moment, then disappeared. She climbed fast, then stopped, and carefully raised her head to peer up over the edge.

Slowly her hair, forehead, and eyes emerged. She looked back and forth across the mesa, but there was no fox.

She climbed the rest of the way to the top, slipped the waterskins off, and looked over the edge at the creek where it meandered like a great snake through the cottonwoods. She could see where she had filled the waterskins and the trail that twisted through the thistles and up through the cliffs to the rock where she fell.

And then the strangest thing happened. She saw a little girl wearing a plain muslin dress a lot like hers and carrying two waterskins. The girl slipped on the loose rocks, fell, and slid over the edge. Sarah called out to her, but the girl saved herself by grabbing a thistle stalk. Then she pulled herself up and stood on the trail pulling the stickers from her hand. The girl surveyed the trail below for a moment, turned, adjusted the waterskins, and looked up toward the mesa.

At that moment Sarah realized she was looking at herself. But herself on the trail did not seem to see herself on the mesa. Instead, the Sarah on the trail was looking at the place where the fox had peered over the ledge before.

She suddenly understood something very strange and a little frightening: She had just seen herself through the eyes of the fox.

She heard a voice that came from everywhere. The voice seemed to take her over. It said: "What kind of water is this that rains down and struggles up?"

"It's water hard earned," was to be her response, but there was no one else on the mesa.

Standing at the very edge of the mesa, she turned a complete circle searching for the source of the voice . . . and stopped. Only a few feet away, sitting right where she had seen him before, was the fox. But now he was looking at the waterskins, full and round, at her feet.

6

THREE
TIMES ROUND

§ § §

The fox twitched. They stared at each other. He winced. "She can see me. Yes, she sees me. She thinks I am . . . she thinks I am a fox."

Sarah heard all of this, but not with her ears. The words she heard seemed to be everywhere at once, because they came from inside her own head.

She peered down at him: "Is that you talking?"

The fox tilted his head slightly and gave her a long, thoughtful look. He was perfectly still and somewhat transparent. He was not exactly a full and solid fox, but nonetheless, he seemed to be a fox. She could hear a low, sweet voice that felt like soft black sand sliding through her head. The voice said, "I cannot talk."

"You talked. I heard you," she replied, in a perfectly normal, everyday sort of way. She looked right at the fox and he looked right back.

"No," said the voice in her head. "I have no words. I have thoughts—perhaps you make these thoughts into talking with words."

"But I don't hear your words in my voice. They're in a strange voice inside my head." She studied his eyes. "Besides, if foxes don't have words, how can they think?"

"I think from the middle of my middle. I don't need words, and I'm not a fox."

"Well, you look very much like a fox."

"That is a misunderstanding about which I can do nothing."

She looked down, thinking of her navel, and asked, "How do you think from the middle of your middle?"

"Not the middle of your tummy, the middle of your mind. No. That's not exactly it either—your words do not say . . . what my thoughts . . . think."

"Is the middle of the middle the most important part?"

"Yes, but there are other most important parts as well."

"My great-grandmother says the most important part is called the soul. How can there be more than one most important part?"

"You need all your parts to be you. They are all most important parts."

"Do you know what a soul looks like?" she asked. "Does mine look like other people's souls?"

"Some thoughts are not said well with words. Can you see thoughts in things?"

"What are thoughts in things?"

"If you come this way again bring me something three times round and I will show you hidden thoughts."

His nose twitched. His coat shimmered for a moment, then glowed slightly before he became completely transparent and disappeared.

"No. Wait, don't go," she shouted. "What is something three times round?" She patted the rock where he had been, then peered over the edge. No fox.

"What is your name?" she called. Still no fox.

She sat on the mesa and wondered at the mystery of the foxlike creature whose name she did not know. She smiled in simple delight. His request for something three times round began to spread through all her thoughts until it filled her mind.

A large blue lizard basked in the sun on a rock near the juniper trees. He blinked at Sarah. She sat quietly on her own rock and studied the white, billowy clouds above the junipers. Today the clouds were full of horses, but none were three times round.

When she got home she gave each plant a careful drink from the waterskins. She frowned at the greedy ground.

§ § §

Lilly slept, curled like a squirrel.

For several minutes Sarah watched her. She examined the two short coarse hairs that grew from a small mole hidden in the wrinkles near the eyelid that twitched. She patted her crooked hand and then lay down beside her.

Sarah's eyes searched the house and the places she liked best: the shadow patterns made by the afternoon sun, and the faces of animals and people carved in beams and cupboard doors. But there was nothing three times round.

Then she quietly named all the things she could think of and pondered the mysterious fox with his strange request. And what did he mean by hidden thoughts?

Whatever was hidden she knew must be hidden inside something three times round. But where can that be? As she considered this puzzle her thoughts gradually took on the shape and feel of particular things: weeds with long stalks in the wind, water soaking into the dark earth, smooth wet stones in a bowl. Gradually a solution simply formed itself out of all the shapes and feelings in her mind. And then, after a very long time spent searching around for the right words, she realized that it must be something that's itself inside itself. Over and over again. This thought left her with an odd sensation, like a feeling from an old memory after the memory was gone.

ᚷ ᚷ ᚷ

The Triune from Henrytown, high-minded and dutiful, with their strange pale skin, rode through the shadows and the light that streamed down between the leaves of the cottonwood trees. The sun flashed from their many mirrors. Leather fringe for flies hung from the stiff, flat brims of their hats, and masks-against-evil hung from their wicker saddles. Kreel and Greyling Eyes carried bullwhips coiled over their shoulders and across their chests. Henkel's weapon was his wicker desk and cargo of record books. Several tin cylinders clattered a muted chime in time to his horse's stride.

The three earnest men were contorted to fit their awkward saddles, and the expressions on their faces said they had ridden many hard miles.

ﺥ ﺥ ﺥ

Lilly opened her eyes and smiled at the child, who was deep in thought about the nature of things within things.

Sarah's eyebrows bunched together in the search for something three times round. She saw Lilly was awake and asked, "Is there something that's itself inside itself, over and over?"

The weathered old woman sat up and stared out the window, looking for a memory. She thought about the child's strange question, then she smiled and said, "When I was very small—only a baby—I woke from a nap and I had a feeling that came all over me. It said: 'Here I am again.' It was like finding the me inside myself. I knew I was me."

"Here I am again?" Sarah asked.

"Yes. It was like being born into life, but at the same time I vaguely remembered my old self before I fell asleep, so it felt like I was being born into a new self."

For a moment Sarah was lost in her thoughts, then she said, "Every time a baby wakes up it feels like it's left its old self and is reborn in a new self, doesn't it?"

"Yes, I think it would. Over and over again," Lilly said, considering the implications. She pulled herself up and leaned back against the window frame.

Through the thick glass, white fox-clouds billowed up above the distant mountains.

"How do you know," Sarah asked, "when you're imagining something and when it's real?"

"I cannot tell the difference. I never could. But that's a secret, never tell a soul," she said, and smiled a conspirator's smile. "Do you think you've imagined something?"

"Well, there's a fox—he's not really imaginary—but he's not really real either."

"What makes this fox so special?"

"He talked to me."

"Really?"

"Yes. And you know what else? He thinks from the middle of his middle, and when he has thoughts I hear words in my head."

Sarah could see that Lilly was confused. She tried harder, telling everything slower and as clearly as she could. "See, he thinks thoughts and I hear words. But he doesn't have words. He just has thoughts. So he doesn't really talk."

"I see."

"And I saw things I never saw before. I could see me the same way he saw me . . . with his own eyes."

"How was that?"

"When I fell coming up the trail. . . ." Sarah suddenly realized she had said too much. "Maybe it was just an imaginary fox and not for real."

"Well, did you really fall or . . ."

Sarah was saved from answering by the sound of horses and men's voices coming toward the house. She jumped up, ran to the door, and threw it open.

The men of the Triune, perched on their high wicker saddles astride their fat horses, towered above her. The flash and glare of their mirrors made their shapes dark in contrast, unknowable as phantoms.

Kreel held a mirrored medallion in his hand and flashed the sun into Sarah's face. He studied her closely for a moment then asked, "Are your parents home, child?"

"No."

Kreel's eyes narrowed and he aimed the light past her into the house. "We are looking for a poacher. Do you know what a poacher is, child?"

"No."

He dismounted, stiff and in pain from riding. "We are looking for a man who killed a sheep. Now what made him a poacher is this: That sheep did not belong to him. He killed another man's sheep. And it is our intention to punish him severely."

Lilly's gnarled hand grasped the edge of the door and pulled it back. She looked up and blinked into the flashing mirrors.

Kreel glared at the old woman and then the child. "You lied to us, child. You said you were alone."

"You asked about my parents. This is my great-grandmother. I did not lie."

Sarah stared up at the man. He glared back. Adults did not talk back to this man, much less children. Finally he spoke to Lilly. "The child has bad manners, Great-grandmother. You must correct her behavior. Do you know of us?"

"I don't believe I do. Tell me who you are."

"We are the Triune, the people's will. That is Henkel, Keeper of Records," he said, pointing to Henkel, who nodded his heavy face in her direction. "That is Greyling Eyes. And I am Kreel. I am in charge. It is our duty to punish those whom the people feel deserve punishment. Today we are looking for a killer of other men's sheep. Have you seen anyone hereabout suspicious?"

"Anyone suspicious? I'm not sure. Three men came," replied Lilly.

Kreel nodded and Henkel struggled with one of the great thick books jammed in his saddle bags. Everyone waited patiently. He managed finally to free the book, lay it open on the wicker desk, and begin writing. He gestured with his quill for Lilly to continue.

"They carried long black whips," she said. "One had a saddle made for writing words. They wore many mirrors." At this Lilly's eyes grew unusually large. She blinked and very slowly a great grin spread across her face. She and Sarah looked at each other. They giggled.

The dirt at their feet exploded with the crack of Kreel's bullwhip. They clutched each other in shock, but expressions of glee were still fixed to their faces.

Kreel commanded: "Search this place. Something strange is here."

Greyling Eyes jumped down from his horse and brushed past the child and the old grandmother to search the house. They followed him to watch, puzzled by the man's strange behavior.

He poked under things, glared intensely, made small pony-snorting noises, examined the carvings on the cupboard, and rummaged nervously through the clothing trunk. This made Lilly laugh. "You must be looking for a very small poacher," she said to the man with his head buried in clothing.

Greyling Eyes looked up, surprised for a moment, then glanced back at the trunk, snorted his disgust at the old woman's teasing, and pointed to the cupboard carvings: "Why are animals all over this house?" he demanded, obviously disturbed by deeper feelings than those aroused by the playful deer on the cupboard doors or the raccoon face looking down from the beam above. He felt trapped in this house. The strange child stared at him. Invisible fingers seemed to close around his throat. His seeing blurred at the edges and in the blurry places he saw things creeping, sliding, and jumping, and he realized the room was losing its shape and the animals on the beams were moving closer. When he looked directly at one of them it stopped, but while his gaze was fixed on one, the others all around made little jumps, bounded, or slithered toward him.

Greyling Eyes screamed. He was a brave man, but he screamed. He opened his mouth and screamed the scream of his life. But no one could hear him because there was no air in his lungs to make the sound of screaming. He reached up to attack the small, sweet raccoon face, tearing at it with his fingernails.

Lilly and Sarah stared, bewildered and confused by his desperation. "What are you doing?" the child asked.

The simple, direct tone of her voice broke the grasp of the invisible fingers that clutched his throat, and the strange man stopped his frantic flaying. He filled his lungs, again and again, in gulps and gasps. His body trembled. He looked at the animals, who were peaceful and still, and at the old woman and the child, who stood quietly and watched.

"Something strange is here . . . demons had me," he said to himself. He backed away toward the door, keeping his eye on the child, but his heel caught and he sat hard on the floor. His eyes stayed fixed on her while his hands felt for the cause of his fall. The feel of the cool, smooth floor made his heart pound.

He kept his eyes on the child and used his hands to scoot himself backward toward the door and out into the yard, into the bright sunlight.

The sun reminded him of his life, and of Kreel. Already he realized that the demons in the house were his and not the child's. And now he was sitting in the dirt with his back to the man in charge. He dared not be a fool before Kreel. He stifled the urge to see if he was seen. Carefully he regained his feet, but as he turned he was met with the flash of bright mirrors and Kreel's dark voice. "Tell me," Kreel demanded. Before Greyling Eyes could speak Kreel pointed toward the shed and said: "Put it in the book."

Greyling Eyes followed Kreel toward the shed. Cool relief flowed from his head to his boots—Kreel, he realized, had blamed the child for his strange behavior. He needed only to say what was expected.

In the shed Henkel examined Aesa's blacksmith tools, considered their value, and made entries in a thick, gray book. When he saw Kreel and Greyling Eyes coming he pulled the appropriate book from the leather bag and opened it to the appropriate place. He was ready. Kreel nodded and Greyling Eyes began telling of his narrow escape from the demons in the farmhouse—demons controlled by a demon child.

"First I felt them in the air. Then they took the form of animals and crawled along the walls. One clutched my throat, another blurred my eyes so the others could attack. Some made small jumps, some bounded, others slithered toward me. One in the shape of a raccoon attacked. I fought back and called for help, but no sound came out. Then, at the child's command, they stopped. But as I left they tripped me and I fell. I could not stand and pushed my way along with hands."

Sarah watched from the door of the farmhouse until Lilly pulled her back inside. They left the door ajar and peered out, wondering what would be next.

Henkel's eyes narrowed. He began turning back the pages of his book, reading here and there. He paused for a moment and glanced toward the farmhouse. Then he resumed his search. Finally his attention was drawn to a particular passage, which he read with great care. He looked at Kreel and beckoned.

They conferred in whispers. Henkel referred to his book, jabbed at a passage with his stubby, ink-black finger, and shivered slightly in delight. At the top of the page several short and tightly written notes accompanied Henkel's drawing of the rainmakers' machines. But in the lower right of the page was the Lizard Woman's description of a child who brought a dead fox back to life, and next to this was the drawing of the fox scratched in dirt. Henkel jabbed his glee at the words. Kreel simply nodded and watched the farmhouse. He walked out into the yard and called to Lilly, "Great-grandmother, where is the child's father?"

Lilly peered out at him. His mirrors flashed back at her. She knew she must say something. Finally she said, "Working his trade elsewhere."

"Does his wagon have high iron wheels?"

"He's too tall to be your poacher," was her final word on the subject of her grandson.

Kreel walked to the well, dropped the bucket, and pulled it up for a drink. He thought about the events of the afternoon, and considered what questions the Lizard Woman and the town council might ask. He paid attention to these small things.

He set the bucket down and walked to the farmhouse followed by Henkel. Lilly peered at him from behind the door, keeping well out of the light.

"At the edge of the field," Kreel said pointing toward the hill, "there is a stone with writing on it. What is the meaning of that?"

"The child found it," said Lilly. "It's a gravestone, maybe. From longago people. Yellow Sailors, maybe."

Henkel wrote with fierce concentration, getting it right.

Cautiously Kreel pushed the door just enough to see Lilly's face. "Yellow Sailors?" he asked.

"Yes. The ones that grew the small white flowers on the mountain tops."

Kreel did not know what to make of this old woman. He stared at her. Henkel wrote.

"For now, we're done," Kreel said.

Greyling Eyes and Kreel, mirrors flashing, mounted their horses and rode off without a word, the Keeper of Records trailing behind.

Lilly and Sarah stood in the doorway and watched the Triune ride away. To Sarah they were a puzzlement. "What does it mean to be the people's will?" she asked.

"They speak the people's mind, and the people hereabout are mean-minded," said Lilly.

"Why are they mean?"

"They are full of fear, I think. When people forget who they are, then fear seeps in. But what they fear, I don't know."

High plumes of dust, illuminated in the late afternoon light, trailed up behind the riders who slipped from sight, though their plumes remained and drifted across horizon's edge like pale, anxious ghosts.

§ § §

Close together on the bench beneath the window-light, Lilly wove and Sarah watched. Lilly, crouched before the loom, pushed the shuttle through its warp, pressed the thread down and tight, and in place of memory recounted colors in a row.

"How do you know what color to put next?" Sarah asked her.

"It's part of the pattern."

"Where is the pattern?"

"This is the pattern," said Lilly, ticking the colors with a crooked finger, "Yellow, blue, yellow, yellow, blue."

"I mean, where does it come from?"

"It's in my mind. I see it in my mind."

"Is it some kind of secret seeing?"

"It's seeing a story underneath the words. It's something like hearing your own music inside your mind."

Water boiled in the black pot, received three eggs from Lilly's crabby fingers, and cooled to a simmer.

A large mouse, carved in the beam above the stove, watched the two make dinner. Lilly hummed and sliced bread and cheese, and Sarah stirred the porridge.

As she ate her dinner, Sarah's thoughts wandered, searching the room. She struck her boiled egg with a knife to break the shell, and as she examined the egg her expression changed from serious to delighted.

"What is it, child?" asked Lilly. "What have you found?"

"It's three times round! The egg! It's three times round!" Sarah cut the egg through, exposing its three circles of shell, white and yolk. She was enchanted with her discovery. She peered closely at the cut egg.

Gradually her expression became a question. "How could thoughts be hidden there?"

"Has your fox hidden his thoughts in an egg?"

With a serious face Sarah considered her egg. "He said I should bring him something three times round and he would show me thoughts hidden inside. Maybe I shouldn't eat it?"

"Take him another, he'll not care," Lilly advised.

Sarah looked at her for a moment, then took a pinch of salt from a small blue bowl, sprinkled it on the egg, and smiled.

And Sarah wondered—does she know?

7

MARISHAN BORISAN

§ § §

Sarah moved quietly past Lilly, out of the house into the faint morning light. She carried a bundle and, across her shoulders, the empty waterskins tied with a yellow sash.

The goats peered over the edge of the roof as she walked down from the house toward the cliffs and disappeared into the juniper trees. She stopped near the place where she met the fox, unwrapped the bundle, and took out two speckled eggs, a small loaf of bread, and a lump of cheese. She sat down to eat, leaving one egg for the fox's lesson. In the dim light she spotted the blue lizard and threw him a large piece of bread. He waddled, lunged, and swallowed it whole. Nothing escaped. He blinked his knowing lizard blink.

She found a small stone, stood up, cheese and bread in hand, peered over the edge of the mesa, and tossed

the stone into the dark valley. After a moment it rico-
cheted off the rocks below. She waited for the fox
until the sun rose over the mountains and illuminated
the mesa in a pool of warm light.

But still there was no fox. She finished her bread
and cheese, slipped the yellow sash over her head, and
slowly descended the twisting trail.

At the bottom of the trail she searched along the
base of the cliffs for a new way to the creek. She discovered a place with high grass and, rising out of the
grass, large round boulders and several beautiful trees
with delicate white bark and perfect green leaves. This
place was unlike any other. Even the air, as it touched
her face, felt unusual. She stood quietly in the strange
meadow until she noticed a break in the grass and discovered a hidden path that led toward the tall cottonwood trees and the underbrush along the creek.

In the highest branches of the cottonwoods, the
leaves caught the morning sun, reflected it down into
the dark green underbrush, and revealed several large
creatures sleeping in a thicket.

Five deer rose up and stretched their long bodies.
They watched Sarah approach. She came quite close,
stopped, stood quietly, and waited. The deer and the
girl studied one another. Their large, delicate ears and
dark, mysterious eyes delighted her. She wondered
how creatures so delicate could be so strong. The

deer raised their heads and sniffed the air for her scent. A not disagreeable odor, it was decided. They moved closer, necks outstretched, sniffing, one step at a time.

Bound by curiosity and some fear, she held her ground.

The deer emerged from the thicket and grew large. Suddenly she was surrounded by their huge ears, beautiful large eyes, and wet black noses that twitched.

They licked her. They licked her arms, her neck, and then they licked her face. She held her breath and squinted. Finally she could hold it no longer and let out a rush of air. The deer jumped back, surprised. Then, pretending insult, they put their heads into the air and bound away as deer will do.

She put her hands to her face and rubbed the deer licks away. She looked across the meadow to where the deer had stopped to graze. One turned to look, seeming almost translucent, and faded away, only to reappear, grazing several feet from where it had been a moment before.

This magical display made her feel so strange that she put her hands to her face and inhaled the deer scent. Satisfied that the deer were real, she continued on her way to the singing creek.

The leaves, the underbrush, and tall grass cast a pale green light along the creek. The fish beneath the bank caught the mottled light and flashed away from the gape-mouthed, goat-skin monster maneuvered by the child seeker of water.

Heavy with waterskins she climbed the path through the cliffs until she came to a white clay bank just under the mesa, where she noticed something she had not seen before—several small holes or burrows cut back into the hillside, with a miniature trough beneath each one. She stopped and peered into one of the strange dwellings. Something in there with a long, thin beak moved back out of reach, leaving a small mystery behind. She peered into the other burrows only to find other small mysteries. She let them be and continued her climb to the mesa.

Hoping to catch the fox unawares, she peered over the mesa's ledge. The perfect, speckled egg waited there, but no fox. Disappointed and a little disgruntled, she climbed the rest of the way to the top and set the waterskins down. The deer grazed at the edge of the small meadow where she last saw them. Inside her head she heard the fox. "You've made some friends, I see."

Sarah saw him sitting in his old place, looking down at the deer. She was pleased. "They licked me," she said. She smelled her arms and looked at the fox with a self-satisfied smile.

"What should I call you? Do you have a name?" she asked.

The fox was slightly charmed by her question. "The thought had never occurred to me," he said.

"You don't have a name of any kind?"

"I've always been a part of other things. So I'm not really a thing, not even the fox you see."

"If you're not a thing and you're not a fox, what are you?"

He was silent for a moment, and then the words gradually collected in her mind:

"I am a pattern ... of ways ... of becoming. I help things to change and become what they need to be."

"What kinds of things?" she asked.

"Anything that changes—that grows up or dies away," he replied.

"What do you do?"

"Whenever something changes there is a small space between the memory of what it was and the hope of what it will be. I am a kind of pattern in the tiny space between memory and hope."

"Do you hold them together?" she asked.

"Yes, in a way, because hope has to remember what it was or it would get lost and nothing would turn out right."

She began to realize how important a part of things he was. "Without you there wouldn't be trees or flowers or clouds or much of anything."

"I hadn't thought of it like that. What I do is what I do."

"Could you show me how to become a flower or a tree?" she asked.

"Maybe. Usually I help things to grow up to be what they mean to be. As a rule they never think to be something else than what they are."

She was very pleased with this fox. "Can you make a name for me to call you?"

He looked at the clouds for inspiration: "Call me Marishan . . . Borisan . . . the Fox."

Slowly she said his new name: "Mar-i-shan Bor-i-san?"

"Yes, just for you."

"Thank you very much, Marishan. My name's Sarah. Oh, yes, I almost forgot."

She got the speckled egg and brought it over to him, setting it on the ground between his paws. She stepped back and observed him for a moment.

"I brought you something three times round," she said, hoping it would suit his needs.

"Hmm?" He considered the egg for a some time. Finally he said, "Could you make it work?"

"Make it work?"

"Yes," he said. "How do you make it three times round?"

She was quite pleased with herself: She understood

and he did not. And she could see him guessing—three perfect speckled eggs in a row? No. And when he imagined the egg broken open, it spilled out on the rock. "Oh, no," she said. "It's not like that at all." Then she realized that he did not know about boiled eggs.

She took the egg in her hand and struck it with the knife. The fox flinched, surprised or maybe sensitive. She turned the egg and hit it again, then cut through revealing the hard-boiled white and the yellow yolk.

He was delighted. "How wonderful and clever."

"Have you never seen a boiled egg before?"

"Never before," he said. "This is my very first. Are they all like this?"

"If you boil them long enough. The yolk is runny when you don't. Can you show me the thoughts in it?"

Marishan touched the half egg with his paw. "Thoughts in it?" His voice was slow and confused. He, obviously, had forgotten everything.

She grew indignant: "You said that if I brought you something three times round you would show me hidden thoughts to think."

"Really?"

"Don't you remember? I wanted to know what my soul looked like and you . . ."

"Your soul, of course—hidden in something three times round. The egg will show you where your soul is hidden. The parts of the egg are like your different selves."

"Like my good self and my bad self?"

The fox did not seem to understand. He looked at her and tilted his head. "Like your outside self and your inside self," he replied.

She picked up a half egg to examine it, when in the distance she heard the bleating of goats. She realized she had forgotten something important.

"The goats! I forgot to milk the goats. I must milk them now. Can you tell me about my soul while I milk goats?"

"Milk goats? What are milk goats?"

"Come and you will see."

She picked up her bundle and the waterskins and started up the path through the juniper trees. As she emerged from the junipers, she looked around, but found no fox. She stopped and called to him, "Marishan?"

He reappeared, sitting in the path ahead of her. He looked at her and she heard him say, "Yes?"

"Oh. There you are."

As she began walking he became transparent and disappeared again. Startled, she stopped and he reappeared, sitting on the path, his head turned back toward her, watching.

"Very well, then," she said and continued up the

path through the sage. And Marishan disappeared
again.

§ § §

Sarah peered around the side of the house looking
for Lilly, but the yard was empty except for three chickens. Marishan reappeared beside her. He observed the
chickens. She looked at him.

"You don't eat chickens, do you?"

"I couldn't think such thoughts. I don't even eat."

He disappeared and she crossed the yard to the
shed.

Lilly was kneeling beside Silas Goat, trying to make
her stiff, gnarled hands pull a stream of milk from the
goat's swollen udder.

Sarah looked at Lilly and at Lilly's hands. Tears
brimmed on Sarah's eyelids.

Lilly looked up and smiled when she saw the waterskins. She realized she would have done the same,
whatever the consequences. "You've been to the creek,
I see," said Lilly. "Your waterskins are full." She remembered her plight and held up her hands: "These don't
milk much. Maybe you should finish." She struggled
up from her knees and rubbed them briskly in hope of
circulation.

Sarah knelt next to the goat and began to milk. Her

words were mixed with the splatter of milk against the pail. "I didn't mean to, but everything happened . . . the time went away, and I forgot to remember to milk the goats. . . . I'm sorry." She inhaled deeply to stifle her tears.

Lilly stroked Sarah's hair, then she sat in the straw and held her tight. "Tell me all the things that happened."

Sarah began to tell her tale, but her words became excited and ran together. "Well the first thing was the deer. They licked me all over my face and I could see right through them and they faded away. Then there was a fish in the creek and something hiding in little holes in the cliffs and at the top the fox told me he was a pattern of ways to be flowers. Maybe I'll be a flower, and his name was Marishan Bor-i-san just for me, he said. He didn't know how the egg was three times round. So I had to show him! He almost told me about my different selves hidden in the egg when Silas Goat called me to milk her. Oh, I forgot, the first thing was the blue lizard who watches out on the mesa and who ate some of my bread."

"Well, I'm surprised you made it back at all. Deer licked you?"

Sarah nodded, put her arms to her face and sniffed, then held them out for Lilly to smell. "Deer breath," announced Sarah.

Lilly inhaled. "Definitely deer breath. And your fox Marishan . . . ?"

"Marishan Borisan."

"Yes, him. What became of him?"

Sarah stood and slowly turned, searching for the fox. She stopped and pointed toward the yard. A somewhat transparent but observant Marishan sat still and proper in the dust.

Lilly's little face squinted against the light. She leaned forward and wondered at the fragile slivers of light that floated above the earth. But it would not be a fox for her.

"He's very pretty," said Lilly. "You say he looks like a fox?"

"Yes, just like a fox. And he thinks thoughts."

"Does he have thoughts for me?"

This thought was too much for Marishan. In a twitch and a quiver he disappeared.

"Marishan!" Sarah shouted to the overly sensitive fox.

"Oh, Sarah, I've frightened him away," cried Lilly.

Sarah knelt down by Silas Goat again and began to milk her. "I know where to find him. I'll find him later," she said to reassure Lilly, and perhaps herself.

Lilly walked out into the yard and inspected the spot where she had seen the slivers of light. Bending toward the ground she saw something that made her eyes widen. There in the dust were four small paw prints. She was almost certain that they were made by a fox. For a moment Lilly was in shock, and dismay was ringing through her thoughts. She looked back at the serious Sarah who milked a serene Silas Goat.

8

AN ENCHANTED
WEAVER

၆ ၆ ၆

Far above on the mesa rim in the long evening light, Sarah pointed and gestured, telling Lilly where the deer were, and the fish, and the mysteries in the cliff. Finally she pointed to the place on the path where she fell and to the spot on the mesa where she first saw the fox.

Pink clouds rolled and skittered and fanned out across the sky. A fat pink fish with wings floated above the flat blue mountains.

Below them the creek made its slow meander through the long shadows of the cottonwood trees.

"The path is steep, Sarah, and I am old and brittle," said Lilly. "If something happens to you I won't be much help. Please, remember that."

"I'll be careful. I promise."

Lilly made her way through the junipers toward the house, and Sarah, with empty waterskins at her side, stood on the mesa edge looking out over the valley, waiting for Marishan. Soon she grew impatient and fidgety. She watched the blue lizard. He blinked at her. She swung an empty waterskin from the end of her yellow sash, and called out, "Marishan Borisan."

His name echoed back and forth across the valley until it faded and the air was still.

Then she heard his voice: "I see you are going for water again."

He appeared in a faint glow of light beside her on the edge of the mesa. They observed one another.

"Why did you disappear when I was talking to my great-grandmother?" she asked him.

"The great-grandmother thinks I'm imaginary. She does not hear my thoughts and she does not see me."

"Has anyone, besides me, ever seen you?"

"You're the first human being to see me. Even if it is a fox you see."

"Why a fox?" she wondered, watching his foxlike glow. "Maybe a fox is good to think just like wild raspberries are good to eat."

Then she remembered his promise and asked: "Are you going to tell me about my different selves hidden in the egg?"

"Oh, yes, thoughts in things, the soul three times round. I will tell you while you go for water."

Sarah made her way down the trail and continued her conversation with Marishan, whose means of travel was to fade away and reappear farther along the trail. At one point he appeared hovering near her shoulder, his head down, almost level with his paws, and looked her straight in the eye. His odd posture made her realize that he usually sat up straight and proper, with his back feet tucked under and his forelegs straight, unless he used a paw, as when he examined the egg. This fox did not fidget, slouch, curl up, stretch out, walk, or run. He sat.

"Oh," she said.

"What is Oh," he asked.

"I forgot the egg."

"Just remember that it has a shell, and a white part, and a middle."

She came to the place where the long-beaked creatures lived in holes in the cliff below the mesa. A strawlike beak emerged and tapped the trough under its small burrow. In the darkness of the dwelling she could see a small shaggy face with small, dark eyes.

Marishan peered into the burrow. "They want it to rain," he said.

"Yes. Everything wants rain. Even rocks want rain."

She continued down the path to the valley floor. As

she made her way toward the creek through the high grass, past the large round boulders, and under the trees with white bark and perfect leaves, Marishan began to tell her about the selves in the egg.

"There is," he said, "the outside self, which is the shell, and the whirling self, which is the white part, and the middle self, which is the yolk."

"Your outside self protects the other selves. It makes words from thoughts. It wears a face, eats with a spoon, and dresses in clothes—being what it expects it is expected to be. It tries to be as much like everyone else as it can possibly be. It is the simplest of all your selves."

"I don't think my outside self works right," she said. "Nothing seems simple."

"If you could see your whirling self, you would know how simple your outside self is."

She came to the spot by the creek, slipped the yellow sash from her shoulders, and lay down on the bank and peered into the water. Through the reflections of sky and trees she could see the fish swimming in the pool below. Marishan appeared on the bank next to her and watched the fish.

"Can I see my whirling self?" she asked and looked at him, intent on his answer, for she suspected this self of being the cause of bad feelings and unhappiness.

"Sometimes in dreams," he said, watching the swimming fish as it came and went between reflections of the sky. Then he became slightly blurry, which caused her to look at him even more closely.

"The whirling self is filled with struggle and feeling. When the whirling self is full of fear it turns our thoughts to stones. And when it's free of fear it gives us wings. But the most important thing it does is to tell the story from your middle self."

She pushed the waterskin into the pool until the opening was level with the water and the water spilled over the rim.

"Is the story in my middle self made of words?" she asked.

"No," he said. "It is not like that. It was there even before your first words. It is a very old story hidden beneath all your thoughts and dreams."

She reached back for the other waterskin and began filling it. "Where did this story come from?" she asked.

"In the middle of the middle self there is an enchanted weaver who weaves the story. Once it is woven, it swims up through your whirling self to the outside, but there are so many terrible adventures on this journey that it arrives at your outside self all tattered and twisted—not looking anything like it did when it began."

Sarah filled the waterskin, pushed the stopper in, then slipped her head under the sash and stood up.

Marishan disappeared as she started back toward the cliffs.

She climbed the trail in the dusk. When she came to the place where the small creatures lived in the cliff, she took a waterskin and poured a little water in each of the troughs under their burrows. Cautiously their slender straw beaks emerged and sipped the water.

"Does the enchanted weaver weave the same story for everyone?" Sarah asked.

The fox reappeared just above her on the edge of the mesa. "Some of it is the same, but some is different," he said.

"How do I know what's the same and what's different?"

"Probably other people will tell you."

She climbed to the mesa and looked out over the dark valley at the silver creek that slid through the cottonwoods.

"Marishan?"

"Yes?"

"Since I hear words and see pictures when you have thoughts maybe I see you as a fox because you think you are a fox."

"Maybe I am only a made-up fox that lives in your mind."

And she wondered, do you live in my mind or do I live in yours?

She waited, but there were no words for his thoughts. The fox had nothing to say; he merely shimmered.

"You are a funny fox, Marishan."

They watched the silver stream in the dark valley below.

"It is very late. My great-grandmother will wonder what's happened to me."

"Good night, Sarah."

"Good night, Marishan."

ﺵ ﺵ ﺵ

In the field above the house three dark figures crouched near the slate-with-words. One of them struck a large sulfur match that flared and illuminated the faces of Kreel, Greyling Eyes, and Henkel, Keeper of Records.

Henkel lit a fat candle and set it before the stone so he could see to copy the strange words written there. He had only begun his work when they heard the distant voice of Lilly calling Sarah. Greyling Eyes blew the candle out. They waited for a moment, rose slowly, and stood on tiptoes like black-footed ferrets, peering over the crest of the hill.

Quickly they slipped through the sage, down the hill, past the well to the house. They peered through the window. The child, made slightly demonic by the odd distortions of the thick glass, told the great-grandmother how it had been and what the fox said. Her words made her hands dance in the lantern's yellow light.

Greyling Eyes watched, and Kreel, ear pressed to the wall, heard bits and pieces, words and phrases of the child's tale. Then, like thick shadows they slid from the house and silently crossed the yard to the shed where Henkel lit his candle, opened his great ledger, and began writing Sarah's tale to Lilly as told by the distraught and overwrought Kreel: "She spoke of a fox—Marchan Borchan, who traps human souls in chicken eggs. They cut open an egg and extracted a soul in three parts.

One part was fed with a spoon.
One part was filled with fear.
And the last was blind and . . . had . . . no . . . mind.

Their large, glazed eyes met in the flickering light. Then, when their hearts could take no more, a large hairy thing with twisting horns plunged forward into the circle of light. Kreel and Greyling Eyes scrambled back into the darkness. The curious she-goat rolled her head and leered. Henkel kicked the candle—it flickered once before the soft thud of running feet crossed the night-black field.

৯ ৯ ৯

Lilly kissed Sarah who was deep in dreams.

The emerald-green trout swam in the darkness of the deep pool. When the wide-mouthed monster plunged into the water the trout quivered and was gone in a green flash.

A thick mist rose from the stream, up through the many-colored leaves of the forest.

And the mist rained dream rain.

9

GREEN LIZARDS
DANCING

ༀ ༀ ༀ

In the early gray light the Triune rode through the trees, whips coiled and ledgers ready. Their faces had a fixed, hard look that came of hiding dread under determination. A soft, murky light flickered across their many mirrors. The horses' hooves were hard and loud on the dry road. Soon behind them came the sound of another horse, a long, dark horse, ridden side-saddle by the Lizard Woman with her lizard-skin turban wrapped tight to her head. Her eyes glistened with purpose and anticipation.

ༀ ༀ ༀ

Silas Goat blinked and looked out across the yard. The chickens blinked, and the blue lizard blinked.

Sarah opened her eyes and Lilly lit the fire to cook the grain for porridge.

Under a light blue sky Sarah hunted for speckled eggs, found another almost round red stone beneath the sagebrush, scattered grain for chickens, looked in the well, and went to the shed to milk goats. The goats rubbed their heads against her. They pushed her back and forth.

Suddenly they stopped their pushing. They looked out across the field. But there was no sound and no one came.

Sarah milked Silas Goat. Streams of milk struck the bottom of the pail. The cats waited and the kittens mewed. Sarah aimed, shot cats with milk, and forgot about what did not come under the light blue sky out across the field. She carried her milk to the house.

The old woman and the child ate their porridge. Sarah smiled at Lilly who smiled back with a look that asked, "What is it that makes you smile?"

Sarah thrust a closed hand toward her great-grandmother, waited until she put her hand out, then dropped the red stone into the fragile cup of gnarled fingers. The frail woman made an odd sound that was laughing and then, slowly and awkwardly, dropped the stone into the clear glass jar with the others. Sarah peered at the small white flowers in the jar. They were new and fresh. She drank her milk and watched her great-grandmother.

"Longago people had those red stones," said Lilly.

"Yellow Sailors?" asked Sarah.

"Yes. I think it was."

Sarah walked down toward the mesa with the waterskins over her shoulder. She was lost in thoughts and unaware that behind her, in the field above the house, small flashes of light moved along the horizon.

The creek below slithered through the soft green woods. The tops of the cottonwoods were bright and pale green in the sunlight, almost white against the dark underbrush. And near the creek the deer that licked her grazed.

Marishan appeared beside her as a faint, reddish glow that became stronger and stronger until he was nearly in full fox.

"Is the creek like a snake?" he asked.

"Maybe, sometimes," she replied. "But a snake can think thoughts."

"How do you know that a snake can have thoughts?"

She thought about this and said, "A snake knows where to go and it remembers things."

"Doesn't the creek know where to go and doesn't it remember things?" he asked.

After some reflection she said, "Sometimes I don't have the right words to say my thoughts."

Marishan agreed, of course. "If thoughts were green lizards dancing, then words would be shadows."

"Yes. Just like shadows, because words aren't alive, but thoughts are. Isn't it so, Marishan?"

"Yes, it is."

"And the creek is like a snake because they're both like thoughts," said Sarah.

Marishan was not so sure he understood this. "How are the creek and a snake like a thought?" he asked.

"Because they are able to move without changing their shape."

"Yes . . . just like a thought." He was delighted and shimmered to show it.

Sarah smiled at him and started down the pathway through the cliffs. Marishan simply faded away.

High above a bright blue hawk circled, riding the morning currents of air that rose from the face of the cliffs.

The hawk saw Sarah threading her way down the path. He turned and dove toward the trees along the creek, plunged through the white light of the tree-tops into the soft dark green, skimmed along the creek, then shot out above the trees, climbed higher and higher, and began to circle above the cliffs again.

For a moment Sarah felt the world whirling around her. She stopped near the foot of the cliffs, sat down, and put her hands up to her eyes. She called for the fox. "Marishan? Marishan? What's happening?"

From high above the cliffs she could feel the tumble

and bump of air rising against wings. Far, far below she could see a girl sitting near the base of the cliffs with her hands over her eyes. She knew she was seeing herself as the hawk saw her. The height astonished her.

With hawk's eyes she plunged earthward, down and down through her own dread, past her fear and into sheer and total terror. She plunged into the white leaves, through the dark trees, and shot out over the sharp slivers of light that flashed off the burning creek.

The hawk dodged between the dark green leaves and the black branches that jumped out from the undergrowth along the bank. Sarah could feel the blast and rush of air against the hawk's body.

She could feel what the hawk felt, but she did not think what he thought. She had no say in what happened and had no idea what he would do next.

She knew this was the trick of the fox and she shouted for him. "Marishaaaann!" The name of the fox carried far down the canyon, echoing off the walls of the cliffs.

Then she was quiet. She took her hands away from her eyes, and looked up. Her body shook and she felt cold. She looked around for the fox. He appeared, hesitant, and sitting in the path before her. He was so hesitant, in fact, that she could barely see him.

"What did you do, Marishan?"

"I showed you what the hawk sees. Did you like it?"

"Some I liked," she said, but she was still shaking.

"What part didn't you like?" he asked.

"When I was scared."

"But," he said, trying to understand, "it didn't scare the hawk."

"Well, I've never been a hawk before. It takes getting used to, you know." She was a little wary of the fox and she was still trying to understand what had happened. "I liked being the hawk. I liked it a lot, but I wanted to know what he was thinking and what he was going to do."

"Would you like to be a flower?" he asked, anxious to make things right. "I can show how to be everything a flower is, thoughts and all."

"What kind of flower could I be?"

"Any flower you want to be. Find a flower to be and I'll show you how to be it."

She was very still and thoughtful. She looked at the fox. What he had done seemed extremely dangerous. It was also truly extraordinary. She wondered how different being a flower would be.

Sarah's path toward the creek meandered from flower to flower as she examined each one, searching for the best one to be. She saw small details in the flowers she had never noticed—saw flowers she had never seen before.

She did not see the deer that licked her in the

woods nearby. They stood very still, heads raised, watching the mesa high above.

ʃ ʃ ʃ

Four figures crouched on the mesa rim, dark shapes against a yellow sky. Like a black flame the Lizard Woman flared back from the edge of the mesa, drawing Kreel, Greyling Eyes, and Henkel in her draft. They huddled near her, glanced back for an instant to be sure they were well hidden from the evil child in the valley below, then turned to confront the glistening eyes beneath the lizard-skin turban. Her voice was strange and high—a singsong sound that made her words hang in the air.

"It is important I know everything you saw and whatever you might imagine it to mean. Tell me now, the part about the spoon:

The fox
Scooped the soul
From an egg
With a spoon?

"Is that right?"
Kreel considered her seriously, getting the words right. He looked at Henkel and motioned to the ledger book. Heads together, they puzzled over

Henkel's words, lost in a blur of ink—the work of Silas, the she-goat. Kreel looked Henkel closely in the eye and whispered harshly through a clench of teeth.

"What does it say, Henkel?"

"It says 'scooped.' Yes."

Kreel looked at Henkel with a frightful blend of disbelief and disgust, then he turned and nodded slowly to the Lizard Woman. "Yes: scooped the soul from an egg with a spoon."

"You are not positive of the words?" she asked in her singsong voice.

She turned her gaze from Kreel to Henkel, who responded nervously, falling over his rapid fire of words: "A terrible thing with twisted horns came from out of the darkness of the black night and—and smeared the page as I wrote these very words, Dear Lady. Terrified, I fainted. You may see."

He turned the ledger book and showed her the smear of ink, nodding his head several times in affirmation of the facts.

She turned to Kreel, a puzzlement written on her face. "In your report to the council you made no mention of a terrible thing with twisted horns."

Greyling Eyes was about to speak, but Kreel interrupted to speak for them both: "It must have frightened us so that we cannot remember at all."

Greyling Eyes looked at Kreel in an odd way, in a squint, not believing a word, but held his tongue—the tip of it squeezed between his teeth as though it were trying to get out. But the Lizard Woman's glistening eyes saw none of this. She was staring into space. "This is very significant, you know."

§ § §

Far away in the valley below, Sarah and Marishan contemplated a flower with fat yellow petals that faded to white on the inside with tiny blue spots. "This is the one I want to be," she said to the fox.

"Then stand very still," he instructed. "Think of nothing at all, and I will let you see inside the flower, and once you see you will know if you want to be what you see, and at the same time you will know how to be what you see."

"How will I know?"

"You will know from the middle of your middle."

"Will I come back all right?" she said, unsure he knew what he was doing.

"You will be fine, I promise."

Sarah prepared herself, standing quietly before the flower.

"Oh. You must close your eyes," said the fox.

She closed her eyes and began her journey into the middle of the middle of the flower. She heard new sounds and saw images and patterns she had never seen before. She seemed to travel through the flower and all its parts and could see the smallest parts growing. She saw how the leaves changed the sun from a ray of light into a green river that flowed through veins, how the roots stretched out through the soil and drew water for the leaves, and how the petals opened and closed. The smallest parts grew and changed and revealed their purpose to her.

After a long wait Marishan asked, "Now, do you know what to do?"

Sarah nodded her head slightly then became very still. Now the things she saw were of a different sort. She descended through a whirl of images and feelings that were all her own: her mother, huge Horatio, the well, burlap sacks rotten in the dust, Girkincod and Hairyweed Tibbletodd, Silas Goat, the insistent sun, Great-grandmother's dream snake, three tiny dolls, the robust man with ice, animal masks on sticks, burying a pet kitten, a smoky sunset, red round stones, the small people painted on the rainmakers' wagon, ice-melt drops on her treasure box, the little fox in Henrytown, Aesa getting his head washed, Great-grandmother sleeping, and a dream about a fishcat that smiled a fishcat smile and dissolved into the deep blue of the deep blue pool. The blue dissolved into red-red that turned to thick butter yellow.

Although she was still standing, Sarah had fallen into a very deep sleep. She left her body behind and became the flower.

The first thing she noticed was that the sun made her itch all over, particularly on her petals and the places where they attached. All her parts changed so rapidly—becoming new and getting old almost in the same moment—that she had a difficult time remembering who she was. The air touched her in many more places than ever before and she always felt thirsty because so much water evaporated from her petals and leaves. Plants she realized, were always thinking about the drought.

A slight breeze moved the grass and the Sarah-flower. The deer that licked her grazed nearby. They came closer and closer. One of them sniffed the standing Sarah, lost interest, and continued to graze. She grazed toward the Sarah-flower, closer and closer. Finally her nose nuzzled the Sarah-flower. The deer was puzzled. She sniffed the flower, grew slightly bug-eyed, and snorted.

The Sarah-flower realized that she was in trouble. She felt the world blur and hum and she left the flower to become her old self again.

She opened her eyes with a start and shouted at the deer: "Don't you dare eat that flower!"

The deer leaped over the flower and bound through the grass toward the trees.

Marishan watched the deer bound away. "Next time," he said, "you should try being something not so tasty." He sniffed her. "There is less of you than before. Some small part of you stayed with the flower."

"Is it a part I need?"

"It is only like the flavor of you. It is hardly anything. There will always be more of it than you can give away."

And indeed, when they examined the flower they found it had taken on something like the scent or flavor of her.

"Marishan, there was something like thoughts at the edges of the petals. I could see them."

"Yes, they make the flower a flower—not a fish, or a tree, or a bug. Only a flower."

"Being other things is a little scary, Marishan, but it was beauti—"

A man shouted from across the creek. Barking, yapping dogs chased him.

10

THE RIVER RUNNING UNDERGROUND

§ § §

The man ran near the bank carrying traps, the furious, frothing dogs at his heels. He jumped into the creek, fell forward, struggled up, and staggered across. The creek claimed his traps, but the dogs stopped at the bank. They ran barking back and forth along the creek until they found a place to cross.

The dogs came running and jumping through the tall grass. They froze for a moment in midair, ears afloat like pancakes as their eyes searched for the running man. Then they fell, barking and yapping, into the grass.

The man found a sturdy aspen tree and climbed to safety without a breath left. The dogs soon found him. They jumped against the tree, gouging deep scratches in its powder-white skin. They growled, yapped, and snapped. The wet man clung to the tree trunk just beyond their long reach.

He saw Sarah below, watching wide-eyed in a thicket. The frenzied dogs yapped and slobbered, unaware of her.

He realized the hopelessness of pleading his case to a child, but he was in a panic. "I am just an old poacher," he gasped, "trying to feed my grandchildren and my old wife. The man who owns these woods put his dogs on me. He means to kill me. Please, girl, go for help."

Sarah was terrified herself, and Marishan was, naturally, nowhere to be seen, but she felt sorry for the poacher and angry at the yapping dogs. She stood up and shouted at the dogs.

"Bad dogs. Bad dogs. Go away, bad dogs."

The dogs turned, confused and surprised. Their strange expressions slid back toward their ears in ripples. They became extremely pale. Their legs slowly curled under their bellies as the last faint color in their eyes faded away. They shivered and grew fuzzy all over, then floated up off the ground and rose slowly through the trees. They had become nothing more than small white clouds.

Sarah was amazed. The poacher was terrified. They watched in silence as the cloud-dogs drifted up into the sky.

Pale and shaking, the poacher slipped and thumped from the tree, looked up at the fading cloud-dogs, whimpered slightly, and edged away, one horrified, slow step at a time. Not until he was several yards from the child of terrible magic did his feet regain their courage. He ran. As fast as his feet could carry him, he ran—through the woods and the briars, through the thickets and the rocks into the arms of Kreel.

Kreel pulled him to the ground, but he struggled. He tried to escape, but Kreel, Greyling Eyes, and Henkel sat on him, making escape difficult. Sprawled on the ground, pinned like a bug, he lay motionless.

Bending toward his head the Lizard Woman peered into his eyes. Her strange, singsong voice made his mind shrivel: "Tell us, good man, what is it? What terrifies you so?"

§ § §

Beneath the aspen tree the amazed child watched the cloud-dogs dissolve into the air above her. "The dogs are gone, Marishan. You saved the poor man from the bad dogs."

"It wasn't me," he said in an odd and distracted, distant voice.

"I know it was you. It had to be you."

"What a beautiful tree, don't you agree?" said Marishan, who seemed already to have forgotten the strangeness with the cloud-dogs.

Sarah looked at the aspen tree then back to the fox. "Yes," she said, "It is a beautiful tree, but . . ." She was puzzled. Why would he say he had nothing to do with saving the poacher?

The fox stared at the tree, his head cocked to the side, almost as though he was listening to faraway sounds.

"I think I should be getting the waterskins filled," Sarah said. "The garden will be thirsty soon."

"Yes, yes. Let us go then." And Marishan quivered and glowed and faded away. Sarah watched him go, still puzzled.

The green speckled trout saw the fox reappear above the creek and the fox watched the trout as the waterskin-monster invaded the pool with mouth agape and ready, looking for green speckled trout. So thought the trout. The trout quivered and flashed through the patterns of sunlight and shadows.

"When you become a tree you must remember that tree time is much different from people time," instructed the fox.

Sarah plunged the other waterskin into the pool to fill. She looked up at Marishan. "A tree?" she said. She put the stopper in the waterskin and stood up. "If I am

going to be a tree I would like to be the aspen tree
that the poacher climbed."

"I thought you might," said the fox.

The aspen tree was the most beautiful tree in the
woods. Its pale green leaves cast the sun in endless
patterns over the dark shadows of the gruesome pines.

Sarah and Marishan stared up through its dance of
leaves and light. "How is tree time different?" she asked.

"It's very stretched out."

"Will I be all right?"

"Yes, but don't stay long."

"Well, what happens if I stay too long, and how
long is too long, and how will I know?"

He looked toward the mountains and the sun. He
squinted. "I'll come for you before the sun touches the
mountains. That will be best." She looked closely at
him, not sure that she should trust him.

"It will be fine," he said. "I promise—before the sun
touches the mountains. Now close your eyes."

She wanted very much to be this tree. She looked
at him. He gave his tail an impatient twitch and
cocked his head. Finally she decided, nodded her
agreement, and shut her eyes.

She began, with the fox's help, to investigate the
secrets of the aspen tree. Marishan's thoughts curled
around the trunk, slid along a branch, and found a bird
inspecting bugs. They examined the clever way the

leaves attached so they would shimmer in a breeze.

She was very still. She waited. The slightest of smiles waited. Now her own images began as she descended through the struggle and whirl of her life: sunlight struck the water and flew down the creek, flashing beneath the banks, to discover the green speckled trout that hid among the black roots, waiting. It waited for its supper to sail by: small yellow snails, flying ants, grasshoppers, and wild red raspberries. Lilly's gnarled hand worked a knife into the reddest of beets, Horatio turned to look and shook his head, a kitten walked on Horatio's broad, rain-spotted back, a small red fox ran through the underbrush, Lilly scattered wheat on the skyline and sang a song while the Silas Goat and Sarah Goat butted heads and Lilly slept curled in a ball. The man beside the ice wagon struck another man with a hard fist and sent him to the ground. The skeleton of an ancient fish swam along the face of the cliff, Mr. Fishcat smiled and swam through bright beads of air that rose in shafts of light and an animal mask to keep away evil swam after him. Aesa washed his loam-black feet in a white basin, and the green speckled trout dissolved into the deep blue pool. The blue dissolved into red-red that turned to butter yellow.

When she sensed the moment was right, she left her body and radiated through the tree so she saw what the tree saw and knew what the tree knew.

She began deep in the ground near the ends of the ravenous roots that stretched through the earth, seeking water and the things the tree used to make more of itself. She could taste iron and copper and other mysteries hidden in the soil. But there was something else nearby—the taste of another tree. It seemed to have different tastes from moment to moment.

The tastes moved up and down and through each other—almost like singing. She realized the tree was talking to her. The different tastes were words. There were separate words, but others combined and changed in different ways to make thoughts. The other tree was telling her either something faraway was coming toward them, or something close-by was going away. She was not sure which it was. To see out she had to find her way through the roots to the trunk, then slip along under the bark up to the branches and into the leaves that caught the light and, for a moment, blinded her.

And something very different happened: What the Sarah-tree saw was a frantic world. Her branches shook rapidly in the breeze and the leaves shook so fast they were only a blur of shining light that surrounded the branches.

In the meadow she could see the deer. Their bodies were motionless but their heads seemed to move so quickly they were only dark blurs floating above the grass. Then, in a flick of time, their heads appeared up high, but turned, looking out over their backs, as still as statues. They stared at the spot where the poacher had run into the woods. The deer snorted.

A strange changing-thing emerged from the brush— a large dancing spider that stretched and broke apart until it became five separate gyrations. But the world began to fade from Sarah's view. It grew lighter and lighter until there was only a pale yellow light and the faintest blur of quivering silver-green leaves.

Suddenly she felt a thunder crack. Sarah sat hard on the ground, her mouth open and her eyes open. She stared up at the aspen tree. It smoldered. Something like smoke rose from its branches, but its leaves were still and the air was silent.

She found Marishan sitting next to her. His head was cocked to one side and his ears pointed forward.

"Marishan, what happened?"

"I don't know."

He was staring at something very high up in the tree. There, in the uppermost branches, barely visible through the smoke, was something as yellow as gold. It was a little man—a very old, very yellow little man who peered down through leaves and smoke.

Sarah moved her head slightly, back and forth, trying for a better view. Then her eyes widened. "Yellow as buttercups," she whispered.

"Yellow as buttercups?" echoed Marishan.

Sarah leaned over and whispered, "Great-grand-mother Lilly told me about longago people called Yellow Sailors. She said they were yellow as buttercups. Do you think that he could be a Yellow Sailor?"

Marishan looked up at the little man for a moment, then at Sarah. "What is a sailor?"

"A sailor goes over the water in a boat. Don't you know?"

"In a boat?" said the mystified fox.

"You don't know boat? People make boats with wood and put big sheets on them and the wind blows them across the water."

"Really?" said the fox, more mystified than ever.

"Yes. That's the way the Yellow Sailors came."

High up the little man crouched on a branch and watched them. He was quite intent on Sarah's whisperings.

"There's a Yellow Sailor buried in our field and his gravestone has strange writing on it."

She paused and looked up at the little man high in the tree. Then she remembered another detail. "And you know what else? They had small, red round stones for something, and we put them in the jar with the little white flowers."

The little man began rocking from side to side.

He made a strange humming and clicking sound: "Ooooheee . . . Ooooheee-tah-heee."

Sarah whispered to the fox, "He talks very strange." The little man pointed toward the distant mountains. "Long ago we grew the whiteness of many small flowers on the mountain tops."

"Then you are a Yellow Sailor," she said. "Was it you that saved the poor man from the bad dogs?"

"Oh, I saved the man's poverty from dogs' badness. But be sure to understand: I don't give a pit for people. I only made the dogs go away because they clawed the skin of my beautiful tree."

"Do you live in that tree?"

"My old soul lives in this tree for a long time, even by tree time—long time."

"Were you in the tree with me?" she asked.

"My tree. I kick you out." He cackled. "Only place I can be is this tree. Many longagos the pale people killed me here," he said and pointed toward the ground. "So I go here." He pointed to his tree. "I live here now. Mine."

"Why did they kill you?"

"Their fear killed our bodies so our souls went into trees." He waved his arms at the trees.

Sarah was astounded. She looked down at Marishan, then back to the little man. "Is one of you buried in our field under the stone with writing on it?"

"In the field no one is buried. In the field Great-grandfather made a place for the spirit of the river running underground. He wrote the secret words and put pretty red stones on them. Magic in the red stones made the spirit talk. He called her Mysterious Woman deep under the ground."

"What did she say?"

"She told Great-grandfather the time for putting seeds into ground."

"But how did she know when to put seeds in the ground?"

"She knows the rain."

Suddenly the little man stood on his tiptoes and looked out across the meadow, then he crouched down again and whispered to Sarah and Marishan: "The man-saved-from-dogs'-badness and other people come this way."

There was a slight shaking of leaves and for a moment he was only a pattern in the shaking leaves. Then he was gone.

Stretching from her nose to her tiptoes, Sarah peered through the thicket. Coming straight toward her were the Lizard Woman, Kreel, Greyling Eyes, Henkel, and the poacher, all preoccupied in their world of burrs, brushes, and thorns. She looked for Marishan and found him peering out from a low tunnel made through the thicket.

"Come this way," he said.

She knelt down and crawled far enough into the tunnel so she could not be seen from the clearing. "What kind of animal made such a good hiding place, Marishan?"

"A blue-bristle boar."

"This is not a good place to be hiding, Marishan."

The Lizard Woman emerged from the thicket followed by the Triune and the poacher. They stopped to extract burrs, except for the excited poacher, who ran to the aspen tree and pointed at the gouges in the white bark. "Dogs were here."

Then he pointed at the branch where he had escaped the dogs. "I was there."

He pointed at the gouges again, and back to the branch, then he looked at the Triune and the Lizard Woman. "The child turned the dogs into white clouds. They disappeared," he said with a shudder and pointed at the sky.

They looked at him for a moment, then turned their backs to him and considered the seriousness of the situation. They spoke in whispers.

Crouching several feet away in the leaves and stalks of the thicket, Sarah and Marishan heard bits and pieces of these dark whispers.

Henkel read from his great gray book of recorded fact, "act of . . . fox brought to life . . . made demon eyes . . . drew the fox . . . caused fighting between brothers . . . store destroyed by fire . . . fearless of the whip . . . made demon eyes . . . Hardkeel's well gone dry . . . the farmer Silas buried alive . . . and then the burning pigs."

And from the Lizard Woman, with her singsong of authority: "Last night and now I saw the demon eyes. I know this evil . . . taken here . . . no longer a child . . . not human . . . I know. I see. All evil, all . . . drought and fire. Death and evaporation."

Full and confident of its truth, the voice of Kreel said: "The child is evil. She must be destroyed. Only then will it rain. We will be destroyed if she is not."

Sarah stared, amazed and frightened. She and Marishan looked at each other. "We can go through the thicket where the blue-bristle goes," said the fox. She looked at him with hard looks. "Don't worry," he said. "The boar is far away, exploring for the yellow roots that grow along the creek."

§ § §

Sarah struggled up the trail through the cliffs to the mesa. When she reached the ledge she turned to watch the Triune far below near the aspen tree. They had watched her climbing and when she turned toward them they ran into the woods and crouched in the brush.

Marishan appeared next to Sarah on the mesa. He peered down at the frightened people in the woods. "What is evil?" he asked.

"Evil is when someone is really bad, Marishan. Do you think I'm evil?"

"I don't have thoughts for your words."

"What am I going to do, Marishan?"

The fox looked at her and whisked his tail back and forth. She felt very much alone. "You can't help me, can you?"

The green evening lizards slid along the rimrocks, dancing with their shadows, long and thin. Their long red tongues flashed out to taste the failing light and the new night.

11

THE DEMON CHILD

෫ ෫ ෫

In the farmhouse, under the lantern light, Sarah watched Lilly and Lilly's shadow making bread.

The old-woman shadow jumped and slid across the room playing tricks on Sarah's thoughts, teasing and mocking and pretending to know what it could not. Lilly could see the child's torment and raised her eyebrows to ask a question.

Sarah sighed and asked: "Can you tell when evil gets inside you?"

"It is not evil that gets inside of you. Evil is when caring goes away."

"When you lose your caring?"

"Yes, when you stop caring about the feelings of other people or animals."

Sarah twisted her hair and looked at her reflection in the polished metal mirror that hung on the wall above the wash basin. "If I was evil would I know?" she asked.

"If you were evil . . . would you care if you were evil?"

This made Sarah smile.

"Why do you ask these questions, Sarah?"

Sarah became small and quiet and the room grew dim. After several moments she finally managed to answer: "People think I'm evil. I heard them say it. They think I keep the rain away."

"What people?"

"The men with mirrors who came on horses and a lady I saw in Henrytown who wears a lizard thing on her head."

"If they say those things it's because they're afraid of something," said Lilly.

"What are they afraid of?"

"Perhaps they are afraid it will never rain."

Lilly held Sarah and stroked her hair.

"When are my mother and father coming home?" the child asked.

"Maybe tonight," said Lilly. "Maybe tomorrow." She held her great-granddaughter and wondered what was in the child's mind and what was real.

"Sometimes I think I'll never see them again," she said. After a long time the child fell into fitful sleep. A troubled sleep with troubled dreams.

She dreamed of fire—long flames reaching high into the night sky and the upturned faces of frightened animals. They howled and snapped at the air.

Sarah woke knowing it was dark. She lay still with her eyes closed and listened to Lilly breathe. She was in Lilly's arms and Lilly was asleep. She heard another sound, something soft and distant. The sound faded away. For several moments the only sound was Lilly's breathing. Sarah searched for the sound, slowly turning her head from side to side in the dark house. Then she heard it again, closer—the sound of hooves pounding across the field above the house—closer and closer until they were at the edge of the field, then down the hill and into the yard. The hooves stopped. Everything was quiet. Except for Lilly's breathing. Sarah carefully untangled herself from the old woman's leathery arms and moved toward the door a step at a time. Her eyes searched for the latch, expecting it to spring up and the door to fly open. Then her hand was on the latch. She pressed it and pulled the door.

In the yard, under a pale crescent moon, Silas's old ghost-white horse stood motionless, watching the horizon. Sarah stood in the doorway. The girl and the horse watched the horizon and waited. There was nothing and the night was still. She looked at the ghost horse. His breathing was tight. His eyes were fixed on the black edge of land that pressed hard against the night sky.

Then a single light appeared, then another, and another, until there were many lights moving along the horizon. The horse spooked and ran. His whiteness faded away into the darkness, away from the lights that moved along the black edge under the blue night.

The lights streamed down across the field and gathered near the stone slate with its strange writing.

Sarah made her way up the hill toward the lights. Near the edge of the field she crouched in the sagebrush to watch.

Five people were on horses, the rest on foot. All carried torches. Kreel, the Lizard Woman, Henkel, the large man with a milk-white eye, and several other faces from Henrytown flashed by in the torchlight.

They made a dance with chants and wailing and long cloth streamers set afire. Astride his fat horse in the dark field, Henkel, with candles at the corners of his wicker desk, wrote his words on paper.

Sarah watched a burning streamer float through the darkness toward her. She tried to flee before she was seen, but stepped on a sleeping hen in the sagebrush. It squawked and flapped, flying up into the flare of light. The crowd saw a flash of Sarah and the blur of yellow-blue-red feathers. Hysteria followed panic across the loam-black field. They knew death was flying at their heels.

Sarah ran in terror back down the hill through the sagebrush to the farmhouse.

Across the field, amid the feet that pounded down dry furrows of dirt, an old man, with an old heart filled to bursting, cried in pain, fell forward, and lay face-down and still. The running, thudding feet passed by, and he lay facedown and alone beneath the thin cres-cent of the moon.

Sarah watched through the thick glass window. Her heart pounded with her fear. Small, dark, and twisted phantom shapes moved across the skyline. The shapes were powerful and strange and unnerved her. They had taken the shape of her fear. She could feel them moving inside her chest. She watched and waited.

§ § §

When Lilly woke she realized that Sarah had already gone—having left a pail of goat's milk and sev-eral speckled eggs on the table.

Lilly stood in the yard looking at the morning sky, then she started off across the field. She concentrated on each step she took so as not to fall, for her bones were brittle and would break. She passed near, but failed to notice the old man facedown in a furrow.

৯ ৯ ৯

Sarah walked around the aspen tree looking up into its branches. When she stopped, Marishan appeared next to her. He was looking up at the spot where they had seen the little man. The waterskins were full and lay against the tree.

"I can't call his name," said Sarah, "because I don't know it."

"Maybe his strange words will call him out of the tree? Say them and see," said Marishan.

Sarah looked doubtful, but tried. "Ooooheee . . . Ooooheee-tah-heee," she called to the tree. They waited, but nothing happened. She looked at the fox. "Can you think of anything? We have to know if there's a way to make it rain. It has to rain, Marishan, it has to."

She stared up through the leaves, wanting to cry, but she was hollow and numb. When the leaves trembled she could feel them shaking in her own body.

She looked at the fox.

The aspen tree shuddered. And the little man, almost hidden in the leaves, peered down from the very top of the tree.

"I'm glad you're still here," she said.

He studied them for a moment, then he said, "The problem is, you see, when you move you're nowhere. You have to be still before you can be anywhere."

"I need to know if the Mysterious Woman under the ground can make it rain."

The little man took his time, but finally he said: "The Mysterious Woman is very terrifying. Her words are hidden in the angry wind. It is terrible to see. Better never to see her."

"But does she know how to make it rain?" asked the fox.

"Maybe she knows. But the child could not understand anything of it."

"Why couldn't I?" Sarah was quick to ask.

"The Mysterious Woman speaks her words through the wind."

"Marishan could help me. We have to try, because everything will be terrible forever if it doesn't rain. Please—help us find her."

The little man crouched on his branch and thought.

Sarah touched the soft white trunk of the aspen tree. "You know how terrible 'terrible' can be," she said.

He looked down and frowned. "I will tell you, but you may regret it. You have no idea how terrible she can be. She's very old and dangerous. You must say the right words to fill the air with tiny spirits that shape the world. Only the true spirit of a person may speak to the Mysterious Woman. And remember, you must never look into her face. Now I will tell you how to

call the Spirit from out of the earth, so climb the tree.
Come close to me."

"Why?" she asked, frightened by his command.

"Magic words are secret and must be said in a soft
and quiet way."

She looked to Marishan for help. The fox proceeded
to rise up into the tree in his gentle, transparent way.
For Sarah it was a struggle. She was not used to climbing trees. It was hard work, it took a long time, and the
higher she climbed the more frightened she became.

She climbed until the tree swayed and frightened
her even more. She held tight and looked up. The little man looked down. They looked each other over.
Damp curls clung to her brow. Her face was marked
with white powder from the aspen bark. Close up, the
little man seemed to have a perpetual smile and large
eyes. He seemed very small sometimes. But there was
something about him that made him appear to be different sizes, depending on what he was saying or perhaps on what she was thinking. Whatever the cause,
the effect made her a little dizzy.

Marishan stretched his neck out and sniffed at him.
The little man eyed the fox with an expression of
amusement wrapped in caution and wiggled his eyebrows very slightly. He glanced back at Sarah.

"Magic words?" she asked.

"Yes. And secret, too, remember."

ৡ ৡ ৡ

At the far edge of the field above the farmhouse five men and two women bent down near the old man in the furrow. Slowly they lifted him into their wagon. One of the men, a huge man with heavy shoulders and a bulging chest, held the old man's head in his thick hands. Large tears streamed down his face and fell onto the old man's forehead. The women made a wailing sound and waved their hands toward the sky. The other men patted the still form of the old man and wiped the dirt and tears from his face. Then they bent his stiff arms so they could slip his hands into the pockets of his trousers and they covered his face with a rabbit skin with the furry side down. They stood back and looked at him, except for the huge man who still held the old man's head in his thick hands. The huge man sighed a great sigh. The sigh became a moan deep inside that rose higher and higher into his throat until it became a wailing.

Nearby, Kreel watched, and Henkel wrote. Their mirrors flashed in the sun and a dry wind blew the tassels on their flat-brimmed hats. Kreel looked up at the sun, then across the field in the direction of the house. Anxiety pulled at his face. He twitched. Time and the sun's heat pressed down on him.

A man jumped up at the far edge of the plowed

field above the house and began running toward
Kreel. Dust powdered up from his running feet, leaving a long trail rising in the air behind him.

Greyling Eyes stopped, out of breath, leaned
against Kreel's horse for support, then turned and
pointed. He whispered in gasps: "She . . . she's come
back . . . she's in the yard . . . talking to the old grandmother . . . she pointed this way. They, they are . . .
coming this way . . . now."

Kreel kicked his horse up and galloped over to the
wagon. He pointed and commanded. The wailing
stopped. The people climbed into the wagon and left.
Several men from Henrytown had gathered near the
field and they, too, were given orders. Kreel directed
them, in various groups, to hide in the hills, to watch,
to wait.

֍ ֍ ֍

The white flowers in the glass jar with round red
stones sat on the table where the sun came in. Sarah
reached down into the shaft of light and removed the
jar, flowers and all. She carried it outside.

Lilly watered the garden from the waterskins. The
ground sucked the water up.

Sarah had made a collection of things near the well:
the petrified skeleton of an ancient lizard, seed pods,

the skin of a pidler tong, a doll with a painted wood face, a pit gowler, three monsallie bones, a small rug woven by Lilly, a lunch of bread and goat cheese, and the waterskins. She put these things into a basket and handed the jar with the flowers and the red stones to Lilly.

Wearing large-brimmed hats to protect them from the hot sun, they climbed the hill through the sagebrush.

They dragged the slate-with-words over to the large flat rock at the edge of the field where they stood it on end. There was a groove in the rock where the slate fit just right and made an altar. Sarah counted the number of holes in the circle of words carved in the slate, then counted the red stones in the jar. There were eight holes and six stones. She dug around at the base of the rock and found one more. She poured a little water into a paper packet of blue clay and mixed it into a paste that she used to set the red stones. One was still missing.

Sarah stood and let the clay dry on her hands before she rubbed it off. Then she turned and walked down the hill toward the cliffs.

Lilly made marks with a stick in the field. She worked her way around from one side of the rock altar out into the field in a wide circle and around to the other side. She had drawn a large, meandering snake and proceeded to stamp a mottled pattern on its back with her tiny feet.

When Sarah returned she had a bag of white clay, which they used to paint the snake. Then they placed colored stones in patterns on its back.

"Did you know that trees can only see people if they stand very still?" Sarah asked, as she made a pattern in stones on the white snake.

"No. I didn't know that."

"If the people move around they just get blurry and disappear."

"Really?"

"Yes, and sometimes trees aren't even sure people exist at all. If you're a tree, people are kind of like ghosts."

"How do you know about these things?"

"I got to be a tree for a little bit."

"What kind of tree?"

"An aspen tree."

"Aspens are best," said Lilly in a faraway voice. The high, hot sun made her dizzy. She stumbled, caught herself with the stick, and swayed. Sarah brought her water to drink and patted her arm.

The people of Henrytown hid in the gullies and sagebrush above the field. They watched and waited in the heat. They were anxious and sweaty.

Greyling Eyes watched from the near hills, surprised and a little confused by the way the child treated the old grandmother. He looked over to see Kreel's response. But Kreel was watching a plume of gray smoke rising in the distance.

૭ ૭ ૭

The old woman and the child had made an altar with secret writing, with round red stones in the circle of strange words, and with a great snake that meandered in the field above the altar—a snake with many-colored stones in a pattern on its back.

They sat down on Lilly's woven rug amid the sagebrush and studied the results of their work. They ate their bread and cheese and drank from the waterskin. Marishan, with his back to them, sat on top of the slate-with-words and studied the colors and patterns in the snake. The fox slowly moved his head from right to left while his tail whisked back and forth.

"This is a very good snake," he said. "Have you thought of putting something blue on its head?"

"Blue?" asked Sarah.

"Yes. Blue would be good."

Sarah got up and looked at the snake's head, nodded her approval, and put some blue clay on its nose.

Without even realizing it, Lilly said, "What a pretty fox." The words just came out of her mouth.

Sarah looked at Marishan and then to Lilly. She smiled at the fox, but he did not notice. There were important things to be done. He looked at the sky then back at the pattern of shadows made by the red stones set in the slate. "It is soon time to say the words," he said.

Sarah stood before the altar and prepared to speak to the red stones. Her doll with the painted wooden head, the pidler tong's skin, the pit gowler, the three monsallie bones, the ancient lizard skeleton, and the seed pods were arranged in a symmetrical pattern on the large flat rock that was the base of the altar.

She was just ready to say the words when she remembered the missing stone. "Wait. I can't," she said. "There's the other stone to find."

"But there's no time. Say it now," said the fox.

"But will it happen right?"

"No time, no time," said Marishan.

"But the Yellow Sailor said we must find them all, Marishan."

"Use a red bead from your grandmother's necklace. I'm sure it will work."

"Do you think so? I'm not sure," said Lilly, but she began to take her necklace off. Her arms and hands were slow and stubborn so Sarah untied the knot. She took the largest red bead and set it in place with the last of the blue clay.

She closed her eyes and whispered the words:

It-tee tah.
Oooooo saht tah
Abbe suk aey ssssaaaaaaaaay tah
Gaaa ssssaaay tah
Geee tah gaah
Spirit of the great river
Flowing underground,
Tell the rain we need her,
Tell the rain we're waiting.

In the hills above the field Kreel waved away the flies and watched the small ritual in the distance.

The large man with the milk-white eye ran down a gully toward Kreel, then crawled to the crest of the hill on his hands and knees, staying low and out of sight of the demon child.

Kreel was irritated by the man. "What do you want, Buckle?" he demanded.

"I'm tired of waiting. We should get her now."

"In daylight?" Kreel asked in disgust.

"Yes. Now. If you don't, I'll do it myself. I'm not afraid, whatever she is."

"That's not what we agreed. We'll stay together about this or she'll get us one by one."

Buckle was tense. He crouched, glaring at Kreel. Then he began to notice that something in the air had changed. He looked around, looked at Kreel. They looked at the sky. The sky was growing darker and darker. The wind began. Low in the west, smoke from fires obscured the sun, and turned it dark and red.

12

DRY SOULS

〽 〽 〽

Something strange. A small whirlwind kicked up a dust devil of dry earth and began to move toward the small figures of the old grandmother and the child at the altar on the edge of the field.

The child, the old woman, and the fox stared at the flat, gray sky and the dark red sun.

As the wind came up Lilly took a deep breath. "It smells like the smell of rain before the rain comes," she said.

They saw the whirlwind coming across the field toward them and they were afraid. Sarah closed her eyes tightly and held Lilly's hand. The whirlwind, fierce and roaring, consumed the altar. Sarah and Lilly turned away from the stinging dust, but the dust did not see Marishan. It passed through him and did not sting.

In the midst of the whirlwind a childlike figure formed out of the swirling dust and stood before them.

The wind sang. Sparks flashed from the stones. In the midst of the whirlwind the face of the spirit began to change.

Sarah opened her fingers far enough to peek through to get just a glimpse of the Mysterious Woman. What she saw terrified her even more and she snapped her fingers shut. Lilly stared, astounded by the sight, unable to turn away or close her eyes.

The spirit child on the altar grew older and older, passing through all her ages in a moment. Her face twisted and shriveled until she was ancient, older even than Lilly. Then she shattered—disintegrating to dust, leaving as she came—a whirl of wind and dust.

There was the sound of rain, but no rain, and then a long and terrible moan followed by a thunderous boom that stretched out across the dark field and echoed back like the sound of ice breaking across a lake. Then it was quiet, and the light returned to the sky.

Lilly was still. Her eyes were like glass and she stared into space. Sarah peeked out, then took her hands away from her eyes. The waterskins lay in the dust near the altar, but the snake skin, the doll with a painted head, the seed pods, everything else, had vanished.

Marishan looked up at Sarah: "What the Spirit said was this:

When people stop seeing wonder and beauty
They forget who they are and their souls dry up.
The world, like the people, begins to change.
The world, like the people, begins to die.
Only when people see with a child's eyes
Will the rain come again.

Sarah stared at the fox and a terrible realization came over her. "Marishan, there's nothing we can do."

"No, nothing at all," said the fox.

Sarah turned slowly and looked up at Lilly. Lilly was in a trance, unaware of who or where she was.

"Great-grandmother Lilly? Are you all right?" Sarah asked.

But Lilly only stared.

Sarah stroked her arm and looked into her eyes. "Please be all right," she whispered.

In the hills many strange and frightful animals peered through the sagebrush. The people of Henrytown squatted down, holding their masks-against-evil before them.

Greyling Eyes timidly set his mask aside and watched as the small figure of the child helped her fragile great-grandmother through the sagebrush. They disappeared over the crest of the hill.

Kreel stood with his back to them and watched the dusk-red sun sink behind the flat blue mountains.

ॐ ॐ ॐ

In the last of the evening light Ada and Aesa unhitched Horatio, gathered his harness, and turned him into the corral. Ada looked toward the farmhouse, curious that no one had come to greet them. She called: "Sarah? . . . Lilly?"

The door opened slowly. Sarah peered out.

Aesa and Ada crossed the yard to her. She was standing in the doorway in her yellow nightgown. Quiet tears ran down her face.

Ada knelt down and put her arm around her daughter, and Aesa went inside to find Lilly.

"What's wrong, Sarah? What is it?" Ada asked.

"Everything's wrong," said Sarah and she began to cry, for no one could understand.

From inside the house Aesa shouted for his wife. She found him sitting on the floor near the stove holding his grandmother. Her small dark eyes were seeing the whirling woman in the dust.

Ada looked into her eyes and touched her face and lips. Her old skin was dry and paper thin, nearly evaporated in the heat. "Bring some water," whispered Ada. Lilly's lips twitched and squeezed together.

Aesa crossed the room and reached for a waterskin above the basin.

"Where are the waterskins? Sarah? Do you know?"

She looked up, frightened and crying, and nodded.

"Get them! Now!" he shouted.

She ran to the door, ran across the yard and up the hill to the altar at the edge of the field. But her foot caught in the sagebrush and she fell. Her head came down hard against the stone. She did not move. There was only the thudding sound of many feet running across the soft new field.

Then it was quiet. The people of Henrytown had surrounded her, holding their torches high to see their good fortune. Sarah lay still and quiet in their ring of light. The ring drew tighter as the least brave became brave at the stillness of the demon child. Then Kreel stepped forward, reaching out his hand to touch her. But she flinched, terrified at his touch, and scrambled back.

The yellow nightgown seemed to flare up, then rush like fire at their feet. The crowd exploded, falling backward in panic against one another, against torches, anguish, and shouts of pain.

She fled their grasp—the fiery demon vanished into the black night.

Aesa heard the screams and clamor of the crowd and ran into the yard where he saw the torchlights above the crest of the hill near the field. He ran up the hill toward the lights.

The crowd, in disarray, did not see Aesa until he was in their midst and shouting:

"Where is my child? Where is Sarah?"

They turned and stared, holding their torches high. They murmured. Then Buckle, stepping out of the darkness behind Aesa, struck him hard and he fell forward across the furrows of his own field.

From the doorway Ada could see the torchlights move swiftly across the field and disappear. She called to Aesa, but there was no answer. She was quiet for a moment, fighting her apprehension. She lit a lantern and stood in its warm pool of light and listened. The pounding in her heart made it impossible to hear anything in the soft night air. She took the lantern and ran through the darkness and up the hill.

Aesa's still figure lay in the field. Ada set the lantern on the ground and knelt beside him. He looked like a sleeping giant in the dirt with his arms thrown forward. She lifted his face out of the dirt and turned it to the side so he could breathe. He was so still. Ada wondered if he was breathing. She laid her head on his back to listen for signs of life. She gave a sigh of relief and softly called his name, softly kissed his face, "Aesa?" But there was no response.

She stood, waved the lantern, called out for her

daughter, and waited. The world was black and quiet.

She left Aesa lying in the field and walked back down to the farmhouse where she found Lilly, dazed and sitting in the dirt by the well. Ada collected a bundle of bedding, then went to the corral for Horatio and led him to the well. She set the lantern on the ground and knelt down beside Lilly. Gradually Ada coaxed her up onto the stone wall. Then, very slowly, the old woman crawled onto the back of the huge horse.

Ada held the lantern high so Horatio could see. They climbed the hill to the quiet figure that lay in the field. She placed a towel under Aesa's head and covered him with a blanket. Next to him she made a bed for Lilly.

ॐ ॐ ॐ

The black sky turned a deep blue and the stars faded away with the night. Greyling Eyes and Kreel watched from the mesa until the stars were gone.

They leaned together—dark shapes against the deep blue sky, and Kreel whispered, "If she's not found and destroyed I dread what will happen to us. We must catch her soon before she takes the form of something large and terrible and the people give up."

Greyling Eyes descended the trail, renewing the search for the demon they were so desperate to kill.

The hard, slick bottoms of his boots were not made for the steep path. Before he had gone far he lost his footing and fell, smashing his back and head on the slant rock. He was stunned and sickened. With a determined effort he grasped a long gray pole lying near the path and drew himself upright. He looked back up the trail, his vision blurred, and his head dizzy with hurt.

Gradually his eyes could make out a yellow blur below the mesa. Then very slowly the blur began to change its shape. More and more it began to resemble something human. A cold claw grabbed his spinning mind—the yellow blur was the demon child hiding beneath the mesa's ledge. His head cleared.

They stared at one another for a long moment, then his face began to twitch—a strange little dance between terror and glee. He had found the demon, but now what was he to do? What would she do to him? He moved closer, being a brave but foolish man.

He paused for a moment, knowing that he dare not get too close. He remembered the long pole. Slowly he backed down the trail until he found it. Keeping his eyes on the demon child, he reached down for the heavy end of the pole. He crouched low, his body twisted away from the demon, but his eyes fixed on her. He levered the pole against his leg. With care and balance, with dread and anticipation, he swung the pole in a great arc until it was pointed dead at the child.

Crablike, he advanced in anxious half-steps, antici-
pating sudden retreat. The pole only inches from her
face, he stopped, unsure of what must be done.

Sarah could not move. She could barely breathe.
Greyling Eyes lowered the pole until it was level with
her heart, then he pushed it forward until it touched
her. He hesitated, breathed deeply, prepared his mind
for what must be done, and pushed forward again,
forcing her against the rock. But he stopped short of
ramming the pole into her heart.

He waited for a sign, an indication. Was she a
demon—something inhuman and evil? But there was
no sign, no retreat, no explanation. Only tears. Then
from deep inside near her soul she said his name, but
only a small soft cry reached her lips.

A strange and confused look came into his face. He
winced from pain. The deep, deadly pain in his soul
reached up and twisted his face.

Sarah and Greyling Eyes looked at each other. He
whispered, "You are only a child, aren't you?"

Sarah nodded, unable to speak.

❧ ❧ ❧

Above them they heard footsteps crossing the
mesa. Carefully he drew the pole away and laid it near
the trail. He looked up.

A round-faced man looked down. He wore a tight, leather bowl for a hat that came down to his eyebrows. "Have you found anything?" he asked.

Greyling Eyes stared at him for a moment, unsure of what to say. How could he dare to help her, whatever the Triune's mistake? Finally he waved the man away. "No . . . it's nothing. I fell. Hit my head. I'm fine now. I'll keep the mesa. You can go."

The round-faced man retreated toward the junipers. When he was gone from view Greyling Eyes looked back at the child. Finally he looked away—at the sky, at the trail, at the creek below, anywhere but at the child, who was never a demon.

He climbed to the mesa and knelt near the edge to watch as she descended the trail. Confusion scattered his thoughts. Now he was an outcast like the girl. He was changed forever and the consequences were as terrible for him as they were for the girl he had let escape into the valley below.

Crouching deep in the early morning shadows of the juniper trees, the round-faced man watched Kreel ponder his fate as the demon child descended the trail through the cliffs.

Far below in the valley and hours later, Buckle, the Lizard Woman, and Henkel stopped their search to drink from the creek. Buckle lay on the grass near a

tall cottonwood and stretched his large body over the
bank for a drink—a precarious balance.

As his large mouth reached for water he saw something formless and yellow floating beneath the over-
hanging bank. He twisted his head to see and there,
only inches from his inverted face, was the demon
child. She clutched the roots of the tree just under the
bank where she could breathe, her head barely above
water. To Buckle's terror he realized that one of the
roots was not a root, but a snake, and at that moment
it struck at him. Buckle gagged in horror—the thought
of something twisting down his throat. He slipped forward into the water. His feet thrashed at the air.

The Lizard Woman and Henkel grabbed Buckle's
feet and pulled him back. He gagged and pointed
toward the creek bank, then to his gaping mouth, a
wild look in his eyes.

The Lizard Woman began to shake. "The demon? Is
it the demon?" she demanded, in spite of the fact that
he could not answer.

Buckle rose to his knees, clutching his throat.
Henkel and the Lizard Woman ignored him. They
took fallen tree limbs and jabbed them violently at the
unseen demon beneath the creek bank.

The Lizard Woman struck something. She looked
wild-eyed at Henkel, realizing that she had the demon

child at last. In her haste to see, she pitched forward into the creek, inhaled a lung full of water, and lost her turban. As she thrashed the water, Henkel carefully peered under the bank. The tree limb was stuck in the mud. The demon child was not to be seen.

The Lizard Woman struggled to the other side of the creek. She sat, hunkered and glum, glaring at him with dark eyes set deep in her elongated, and completely hairless head.

§ § §

Kreel sat on his fat horse on a hill overlooking the valley. He watched as Buckle struggled through the brush toward him. Buckle waved frantically with one hand and clutched his throat with the other. Kreel watched and waited, unwilling to go to his aid, but curious of his condition. As Buckle approached, Kreel manipulated his mirrored medallion to flash sunlight in the man's face in hope of a better view.

Buckle reached Kreel and grabbed the saddle for support, gasping for air. A strange and terrible rattling came from deep inside his throat. His face and lips were blue and his eyes were wild and glazed with terror. He clutched the medallion around Kreel's neck, pulling the man's surprised face toward him. Although

Kreel struggled to escape, Buckle had no interest in the man in charge. He believed that something was lodged in his own throat and aimed the mirror to see. In the hazy, distorted reflection of his dark passageway Buckle saw what he dreaded most to see: the unmistakable flicker of snake's tongue.

He released his grip on the medallion and fell to the ground where he lay rigid and still. Kreel dismounted and with some difficulty opened the man's mouth and peered in. He saw nothing, though he moved Buckle's head about and even flashed sunlight down his throat with the medallion. Buckle remained rigid, still, and blue.

Henkel and the Lizard Woman struggled uphill toward Kreel and Buckle. The Lizard Woman was soaking wet, but she had fashioned a new turban from one of her white undergarments. Breathing hard, she bent over Buckle, rolled his eyelid back with her thumb, and quickly stepped back. She grabbed her long-beaked mask with ferret eyes and held it to her face. Then she felt his arms and legs and touched his blue lips.

"He is possessed," she pronounced. "He is in her grip. Destroy him now—before the demon wakes and takes him over."

Kreel looked at Henkel who quickly looked away.

"Henkel, you know what to do," Kreel commanded.

၆ ၆ ၆

Through the distortions of the heat on the opposite ridge a figure could be seen leading a large horse with a rider who had two heads. Then the horse turned and it was apparent that there were two riders. They stopped and looked across the valley at the smoke that twisted up through the curling air. They heard Buckle's scream, high and narrow over the dry hills, echo down the valley. It echoed again and died away.

13

THE DARK TOWER

§ § §

S arah hid in a thicket near the creek where the valley opened wide. She curled up in her wet nightgown, closed her eyes, and fell asleep.

She dreamed of the dogs with ears like pancakes, the way they leapt in the air and froze there, with their ears flapped out like that, and looking. Looking for her. They barked and lunged through the grass. Barking and barking.

It was evening when she woke, and the dogs that barked were not merely dream dogs. Louder and louder, she heard them barking. They had found her trail.

She stood up, looking for an escape. This was a place she had never been. It had an odd look to it. The trees nearby were long and narrow pines. Streamers of dark green moss hung from their branches. On the banks of the creek the stones were

large and white and smooth. A place where people
never came.

She called out, "Marishan. Marishan, where are
you? Please, Marishan, I need you . . . now."

The barking grew louder and more savage as the
dogs closed in on their prey. Sarah ran into the forest.
The rough bark of the long narrow pines snagged and
tore at her yellow nightgown. Sarah ran hard and fast.

§ § §

By the creek near where the aspens grew, Aesa,
bruised and hurting, led Horatio with Lilly and Ada
on his back. They called Sarah's name and heard it
echo in the hills.

Then Ada turned her head and was quiet for a
moment. "Listen," she said, "Dogs. Can you hear
them? Dogs barking . . . far away."

§ § §

Sarah ran through the long dark woods and the
dogs were closer, louder. They blurred brown and
black through narrow trees and long green moss. The
dogs ran hard and fast.

At the edge of a field near the forest there was a
round tower made of long black poles bound with

large hoops and chinked with a dark red mortar. Large wooden pegs spiraled around the tower to the top. They served as steps to a small door just under the roof. Scoops for lifting grain were attached to ropes on one side of the tower. Several feet above the ground and on opposite sides were two small chutes with slide doors for spilling the grain into wagons.

Sarah emerged from the forest and ran toward the tower. She climbed the stair pegs, hugging the side of the tower, one step at a time. She heard the dogs. They came running from the woods. They barked and lunged into the air.

She was near the top of the tower when one of the mob spotted her and the call went out that she was found. The dogs barked and growled and their lips curled back above their fangs.

She reached the small door and peered in. It was dark at first and she had to feel her way. Inside was a narrow platform that seemed to drop off on three sides, but before she could investigate further she noticed something shining in the dark. It had a familiar shimmer.

"Marishan? Is it you?" she asked.

"Yes, it is. What will happen?"

"I don't know."

They peered out the door. People began to collect near the base of the tower.

Marishan watched the people below. Something

inside them twisted and pulled, making them dance a strange little dance. "They are afraid of you," he said. "You must make their fear go away."

"I don't know how to make their fear go away."

"Then it would be best to escape," he said.

"How, Marishan?"

"I could help you be a bird and you could fly away."

She searched the sky for a bird. There were none in sight. "No birds, Marishan, not one," she said, almost as though she did not care about escape, as though she was thinking of something altogether different.

ௌ ௌ ௌ

On the ground below, Henkel stationed a man with a long sharp stick at the bottom rung of the stairs. The crowd clustered around Kreel, who had a plan.

"Draw lots. Who's to flush her out?" said Kreel.

He held in his hands several spears of brittle, yellow grass. Timidly they drew until one of them gasped. He was a smallish man with a mustache and a thin ratty beard. They drew away from him. He held his grass spear away from himself. He stared at the ink-black tip and whimpered. They pressed a long, pointed spear into one hand and a firebrand into the other. They guided him to the stairs. He walked joltingly, stiff-legged, like a boy to his doom.

With his back against the tower he took one encumbered step at a time until he was nearly halfway around and halfway to the top. The mob watched, side-stepping beneath, as he climbed the twisting stairs. With each step they murmured chants and tokens of encouragement. Suddenly a peg cracked. He yelled and fell in a shower of sparks. Several weathered pegs snapped under the weight of his falling body.

Now no one could go up and no one could go down.

Greyling Eyes, who had been watching in the trees, rode toward the tower and into the mob. He stood in his stirrups, holding his hands high to quiet them. They fell silent. He spoke to them in a large voice: "You are all crazy with fright. The child's no demon. She isn't evil. She's a child. Only a child. Try to understand this."

In the crowd the round-faced man and Kreel looked at each other. Kreel nodded and they moved toward Greyling Eyes and the mob moved with them. They surrounded his horse, pressing in. They pulled him to the ground and dragged him around the tower until they were directly beneath the demon's hiding place.

The Lizard Woman pointed upward. A haze of wheat dust, illuminated by the long evening sun, rose like demon's light from the doorway. "Only a child? We see what we see. That is what we see."

He had enraged them. They began kicking and punching, until Greyling Eyes lay unconscious in the dirt. All stared down, seething at the still figure. Except the Lizard Woman. She stood staring up at the illuminated wheat dust streaming from the tower doorway.

Suddenly she grabbed the animal mask that hung from her waist and put it to her face. "Look! The demon!" she yelled.

They turned and stared at the top of the dark tower. In an instant they, too, had their masks before their eyes, for the demon child was looking down at them. The long sun caught the yellow nightgown and held her suspended and floating in the darkened doorway. She glowed like an apparition against the darkness.

A whirling moan rose up from the crowd's collective terror. Kreel knew they were nearly lost. He screamed at them, "Burn the tower! Burn the demon!" and broke their trance.

He ordered several people to fetch wood and straw to make a fire. These surged off to perform their duty. Others shouted oaths and rhymes. One fainted. Some covered their eyes, some their mouths. Several were frozen in terror, their masks-against-evil held firmly to their faces, staring at the demon child floating in the darkness above.

Wind-fallen trees were dragged from the forest. Straw was gathered from the field. These were placed around the tower and set afire. More logs were thrown down directly beneath the doorway. The fire began to consume the tower.

ᔥ ᔥ ᔥ

Sarah watched from the doorway. Below, many small, flat masks stared up, floating above the hard dry fear of the crowd. She felt cold and hot at the same time. Like ice—mountain ice dripping down and steam rising.

"Marishan, could you help me be ice?" Sarah asked.

"Ice? Yes, since you are mostly made of water anyway, ice is very simple," he replied.

"Then I will be ice, Marishan."

"But, if you are ice their fire will melt you."

"Yes. Then I will become a mist."

"A mist? Are you sure?" asked the fox.

"Yes, a mist should work just right," she said in a strangely calm voice.

The fox realized she had something in mind he had never experienced before—something he could not understand at all. "Be a mist and I will always be with you," he replied.

Her smile came from deep inside. "Thank you, Marishan."

The fox watched the frantic crowd below. "Ice.

Now is the time," he said. "I will show you how to be the ice."

She could feel the heat rising. She was still and calm and waited for the fox's thoughts to find the precious ice. His words were round and slow: "Miraculous ice from mount'n caves. Clean and clear. Have you ever seen ice so pure?" The robust man turned and smiled. "Take this ice," he said. "This ice is for you."

The fire licked the long poles of the tower and ran in streamers up the side. The flames reached the doorway and found the large crystal ice that reflected the evening sun and the blue mountains. The flames licked the Sarah-ice and she began to melt. Small droplets rolled down her face and flowed in fine streams to small pools on the doorsill. The pools flowed together, became a single pool that pushed to the edge of the sill, and swelled higher and higher refusing to break, refusing to fall into the hungry flames that licked the air. But water pressed against water until she burst over the sill, and tumbled, and twisted, and fell through the air like rain. The Sarah-rain fell into the burning logs and exploded. She hissed like an angry snake and rolled up out of the fire.

For a moment she floated as a mist in the evening light above the crowd. Instead of waiting for the breeze to carry her across the field to escape the fear and rage of the crowd, she did something both terrible and wondrous at the same moment. She let her own fear vanish into the air and very slowly she settled into the crowd.

And the crowd inhaled her. Deep into their lungs, they inhaled the Sarah-mist. She could feel herself sinking into their souls, like soft particles of light descending through the currents of a dark stream. She was amazed that it was so easy and simple. How, she wondered, could a thing so simple be so unlike anything I've ever known? She felt their cold astonishment as they sensed something sinking dangerously deeper and deeper into those dark and distant places where dreams are made.

She descended into the harsh, hateful whirl of their lives, into the saw and cleaver of their souls, into the hacking and whirling, gnashing teeth and blades, scornful stinging eyes, gossip mouths, bitter words and murderous threats, bloody fists, broken faces, and the torn and blackened bodies of those they had beaten and burned.

From all of this the Sarah-mist drew out the pain and fear, the hate, and the vengeance that for so many years had defined the people of Henrytown and told them who they were. She drew these poisons from their whirling lives and fed them to the fire that consumed the dark tower. The flames turned the air dark and acrid.

The people struggled against the loss of all those things that had named them and given them reason and purpose. Some screamed, some choked and gasped. Their eyes burned and they put their hands to their eyes. In dread of pain they fell to the ground. Some clutched at the ground and cried.

Then gradually they became still and silent for they had gone to sleep.

Marishan watched quietly in the field nearby. "Now the rain will come, Sarah." And he was right. Thunderclouds had filled the sky and rain began to fall on the sleeping crowd.

The rain fell on the dusty backs of the horses. They neighed and kicked the air. The record book fell from the wicker desk perched on Henkel's horse and drops of rain washed away its words.

The rain washed the mist, the Sarah-mist, from the air, from the straw stocks, and from the clothes of the crowd, into small rivulets that flowed into larger and larger rivulets that were soon a stream. The stream meandered until it came to a place near the woods and flowed into an old pond.

Near the tower, people began to awaken in the rain. The rain had washed the drought from their souls and the pallor from their faces. There was something in how they looked and moved that had changed. Some cried, some laughed, some sang, some were silent and thoughtful, and some were insane and incoherent.

Many spoke at once. One asked, "Have I been in a dream? A terrible, frightful dream?" Another said, "Fear had its claw in my old brain." A young woman shouted, "It's raining, Beal! It's really rain."

The Lizard Woman raised her face to the rain. She let the drops wash over her eyelids and her lips, and savored the taste of tears in rain. She stood very still with her eyes closed and smiled for the first time in a long, long time.

§ § §

A large man on foot, leading a horse with two riders, came toward them through the rain. The people became silent. Their eyes followed Aesa as he led Horatio with Ada and Lilly on his back. They were soaked by the rain and they were frightened. Aesa walked up to the smoldering tower, to the people there, and led Horatio among them looking for his daughter.

Ada and Lilly searched the wet faces, but could not find her. Finally Ada asked them what she feared most to ask: "Have you seen our daughter? Do you know what has happened to her?"

In truth they shook their heads or murmured no or watched in silence. Then the Lizard Woman pointed across the field to the pond and cried out, "Look. Look there."

The evening sun slipped beneath the clouds and lit the rain and the peaceful child who stood by the pond, watching them.

Everyone followed as Aesa led Horatio with Ada and Lilly through the rain to Sarah. Ada slid off and ran ahead to her daughter. She knelt down and held her. Sarah watched the faces of the people who had gathered around. She looked into each face and each face looked back. Some in curiosity, some in wonder, and some in puzzlement.

Aesa held his daughter close, then he lifted her high up and set her on Horatio with her great-grandmother. As they left across the field, Ada walked alongside Horatio holding Sarah's foot. She looked up often to be sure her daughter was still there.

Sarah fell asleep and began to slip away, but Lilly caught her and held her tightly.

14

AFTER MANY YEARS

֍ ֍ ֍

The land sloped away toward a dense grove of juniper trees and emerged on the other side as the rock ledge of a mesa. The hidden mesa looked out over a narrow canyon and far to the south and west was a range of high, sharp mountains, solid blue and flat as paper cut out and pasted against the sky.

A child, whose name was Lilly, stood with her mother on the mesa in the evening light. "Mother," she asked. "Does the woman who lives in the earth know the weaver who lives in my soul?"

"Yes, I think she does," said her mother.

Lilly watched the silver creek slide through the soft dark green of the cottonwoods. "And what," she asked, "does this weaver weave in the middle of the middle of my soul?"

Sarah smiled and looked into her daughter's eyes. "She weaves a story that is hidden beneath all your thoughts and dreams," said Sarah.